NeW FicTIOn

MATTERS OF THE HEART

Edited by

Chiara Cervasio

First published in Great Britain in 2004 by
NEW FICTION
Remus House,
Coltsfoot Drive,
Peterborough, PE2 9JX
Telephone (01733) 898101
Fax (01733) 313524

SB ISBN 1 85929 097 3

FOREWORD

When 'New Fiction' ceased publishing there was much wailing and gnashing of teeth, the showcase for the short story had offered an opportunity for practitioners of the craft to demonstrate their talent.

Phoenix-like from the ashes, 'New Fiction' has risen with the sole purpose of bringing forth new and exciting short stories from new and exciting writers.

The art of the short story writer has been practised from ancient days, with many gifted writers producing small, but hauntingly memorable stories that linger in the imagination.

I believe this selection of stories will leave echoes in your mind for many days. Read on and enjoy the pleasure of that most perfect form of literature, the short story.

Parvus Est Bellus.

CONTENTS

Lost Love	Lorraine Middler	1
Torn Between Lovers	Lynsey Tocker	4
My Best Friend's Husband	Susie Field	9
The Sewing Box	Merle Sadler	16
Teenager In Love	Johnny Wallman	19
Meeting Of Minds	Lynda O'Neill	24
Smother Love	Joyce Walker	29
First Impressions	Margaret Webster	32
Déjà Vu	Terence Leslie	36
Four Down Two Across	Ruth Locker-Smith	42
The Third Drawer Down	Thelma Kellgren	46
My First Love	Michael McNulty	52
Flames Of Destiny	Tony Gyimes	57
The Boy On The Bridge	F A C	62
Romance Is A Country	Kirk Antony Watson	68
Two Newcomers	Dennis Marshall	72
Summer Lovers	Christopher W Wolfe	78
Distant Dreams	Martin C Davis	84
Out For A Duck	Maddie Bourke	97
Seasons In Love	Kathleen Townsley	101

LOST LOVE
Lorraine Middler

The sun blazed in the window catching on Hazel's gorgeous golden hair. It was a beautiful March evening and the birds were chirping happily. Hazel's mood however was in sharp contrast to the weather. Her exquisite features looked haunted, her pallor grey as she sat on the edge of her bed remembering - remembering her wedding day exactly one year before.

The guilt was still there, perhaps even more so as she remembered herself and Tony standing at the altar - *her* Tony. She had been so happy - David had agreed that it would be their secret and Tony would never find out. She also remembered vividly the stomach-churning feeling as Tony leant across and whispered, 'I know!' The tears trickled down her cheeks at the thought.

Married life had started badly but it was obvious that even though she had betrayed Tony, he loved her deeply. That feeling was reciprocated - Tony was the only man she had ever truly loved and she had to find a way to make him see and understand this. They had said they would stick by each other whatever happened and she fully intended to hold onto Tony forever.

Hazel was brought back to reality by the gurgling sounds of Sam on the bed behind her. Robotically she picked up her tiny son and cuddled him to her. The tears still flowed but six-month-old Sam was totally oblivious to his mummy's distress. She looked into his big blue eyes and could see his father staring back at her. Sam did not appear to have inherited any of his looks from her - he was his father's double!

Sam was such a good baby - never having caused any problems since the day he was born. Once more, Hazel began to reminisce - back to the day he was born. Tony had treated Hazel like a china ornament since the day he found out she was pregnant. She remembered his words uttered with a tear in his eye when she announced she was expecting. 'Hazel, darling, you have made me the happiest man in the world'. They had hugged each other, cried a little and started to make plans for the future - for the three of them.

The pregnancy had gone without a hitch, no morning sickness, no back pains and Hazel had positively glowed. Tony had looked so proud from the first day and they were truly happy with each other and the impending birth. Hazel had felt the first pains one morning as she lay in bed. Tony had already left for the office, so she eased herself out of bed gently. As she reached for the phone, the pain shot through her body. She tensed herself against the pain and punched in Tony's mobile number. The phone rang twice and then the familiar voice. 'Hello, Tony Vicenti.' When Hazel told him she was in labour, the phone went dead and he was by her side within five minutes. He supported her out to the car, helped her in and raced her to the hospital, encouraging her to breathe all the time.

Tony had sat with Hazel through the whole labour, encouraging her, holding her hand and mopping her brow. When she said she couldn't take any more it was Tony who took control, uttered comforting words of encouragement and ordered the midwives to administer more pain relief. With a final searing pain Sam entered the world, all 8lb 12oz of bawling baby at one o'clock on September 26th 2000. Although exhausted, Hazel was glowing and Tony kissed her as they were told it was a bouncing baby boy. She recalled his emotional words. 'Thank you for our beautiful son'.

A shout from downstairs brought her back to the present.

'Hazel, are you almost ready? The table's booked for eight o'clock and the baby-sitter will be here in half an hour.'

Dinner! The last thing she wanted to do - and on her first anniversary as well. She would be expected to smile and make polite conversation. She rose from the bed and placed Sam in his cot. He made gurgling noises as she laid him down and kissed him lovingly on the forehead.

She crossed to the wardrobe and as she opened it, saw the slinky red dress that he had bought especially for tonight. Why did she feel a pull towards the black outfit? It was obviously to match her mood. She knew better, however, than to annoy him and picked out the little red number. As she slipped it on she knew that she looked stunning - her figure had returned to normal quickly after Sam was born. It was a shame that she did not feel stunning - she felt like an empty shell - frozen in the past!

Hazel took a deep breath - she knew she had to go through with this. She checked on Sam who was sleeping soundly and was jolted once again by those familiar features. She left the room and reluctantly started to descend the stairs. On reaching the bottom she heard the wolf whistle and turned abruptly.

'You look gorgeous,' he leered and swiftly crossed the hallway to kiss her cheek.

She felt herself cringe but reminded herself she was doing this for her son, so that he could grow up with his mother and father.

As they headed for the door she looked up into his face and saw those same familiar features - there was no doubt that Sam was David's son. That is what Tony had seen when Sam was brought to him at the hospital and Hazel had never seen him again.

She was informed that his body had been recovered from the river later that day.

'No suspicious circumstances,' they had said.

Only Hazel knew the real truth, that Tony could take no more and had ultimately died of a broken heart.

As David smiled at her she knew she could never love him. The only man she had ever truly loved had gone forever . . .

TORN BETWEEN LOVERS
Lynsey Tocker

As the lady checked the details on the boarding passes and confirmed the two passengers were present for the 1500 hour flight to Washington, Katherine breathed a sigh of relief, she was finally leaving England. She hoped America was to be all she'd dreamed and she hoped the new start would bring her family closer together.

Her daughter and unborn grandchild were already over there and awaiting their arrival.

Katherine was about to board the plane that would take her to her family, a new life, and closer to her husband. Or so she hoped. What had England given her worth remembering?

Yes a home, a husband, a life as a mother and job, but very little fulfilment. Katherine had spent most of her years living for others. She was a mother, a wife, an ex-manager, but she wasn't the *real* her in so many ways. So many of her dreams were unfulfilled. Her passions put out or dismissed.

But she did have the few short months with Lorna. Lorna had become firstly her friend, then her inspiration, her dream, her hope, and her lover.

Lorna was a secret part of Katherine's life that only occupied such a short space of time in Katherine's longer life compared to Lorna's. Katherine was now approaching forty-six, while Lorna was a mere twenty-four. Katherine was young for her years in both her appearance and ways. She'd always kept herself well, despite the lack of attention from her husband. She wasn't made up or false, but naturally attractive. She was slightly taller than Lorna at 5ft 6, compared to her 5ft 3. She had a toned body from visiting the gym and a very womanly shape as someone once described to her; a guy in some bar who Katherine befriended while her husband was off talking to someone else once again. She seemed to remember the compliment and the sensation it gave her at the time. It reminded her she was a woman, which she often didn't feel these days.

Lorna described Katherine as alive, passionate, brave and fun. Her family knew her as quiet, a dreamer, alone in her own thoughts so often. Lorna was fond of her short hair and the time she took styling it. It was highlighted and always looked so neat. Yet Katherine would simply just run some gel through it in the morning before work and that was it. Then once when Lorna had stopped over with Katherine she had asked her to do her hair. Lorna loved the feel of her hair and Katherine loved the way she touched it and played with it in a teasing way.

Lorna was a bright and attractive young lady. She had curly hair that always looked different shades. In the sun it brought out the blonde and light brown shades; in the artificial light it showed reddish tints; and in the moonlight it just shone, Katherine had said. She had a petite figure and was very feminine in her style of clothes. Often in skirts, dresses and heels.

Lorna was like Katherine in many ways as far as their personalities, but Lorna was the more fiery of the two. If she believed she was right then that was it. She stood up for what she believed in and would do so for others. Katherine had inner strength whereas Lorna showed more courage on the surface. In so many ways they were like two pieces that just fit together.

Lorna had once told Katherine that they didn't need to try, they just worked. They were just at ease with one another and couldn't spend enough time together. Even if they argued over silly things they would then laugh and just carry on.

But now Katherine was leaving. She'd left Lorna a while ago but this final part of going brought back memories and a pain in her heart. Katherine couldn't help feeling sad and alone inside.

The two had met through work. Katherine was senior to Lorna. At first they didn't really notice each other, but then they started to share shifts sometimes and this is when Lorna noticed how good Katherine was at her job. She was so capable, a leader and respected by others. They started to enjoy working together and quickly became friends. They shared many interests, dreams and feelings. Katherine became a good friend when Lorna was feeling low. She would cheer her up, or be there to listen. Katherine would never really give much away about herself though. Lorna just knew she was married and that she worked long hours. However, she sensed there was something missing in Katherine's life.

As time went on they went out a couple of times as friends and really enjoyed each other's company. Katherine was aware of Lorna's sexuality from hearing things at work but it didn't bother her as she had gay friends. They got on great and Katherine was enjoying the attention and company.

However this is when things started to develop. Both women knew there was something more than friendship there. One night they admitted their feelings for one another.

From here on, things developed quickly. Katherine had found something she'd always been lacking in her life. She felt loved, wanted, alive. Lorna re-lit her dreams and believed in her. Katherine felt attractive again and she adored Lorna.

Together they shared a few months that would give them both a life-long bond. Lorna too had never felt this way about anyone. She was completely happy with Katherine and having her was enough. The only problem was Katherine wasn't really Lorna's.

The deeper Lorna and Katherine fell in love the harder Lorna found it to share her and keep giving her back. Lorna wanted Katherine for herself. She knew Katherine was happy with her, but she also knew there were two sides to Katherine. She lived two lives and only one could continue. Katherine had to choose between lovers.

Katherine's husband loved her in his own kind of way, as she did him, but she wasn't in love with him. Her heart wanted Lorna. He could offer her money, stability, the chance of living abroad, normality now and as she got older.

Lorna could offer herself, her love, the chance of making a life together and the chance to let Katherine be Katherine.

The final calling for the three remaining passengers broke her thoughts for a second. It was almost time to go, but running through her mind was still Lorna. Had she made the right choice? Was she right following her head and not her heart? Lorna had kept telling her it could work. Katherine knew Lorna bought out the better side of her. She made life fun and exciting. She made her happy. But could this dream really become a reality? Katherine didn't believe she could give Lorna what she deserved and so she'd told her to follow her dreams and that she'd meet someone more suitable in the future. Katherine loved Lorna with all her heart and knew Lorna couldn't understand her choice of lovers, but she had to make the decision, and she had done so a few months back.

As she saw Lorna get on the train for the last time, she held her hand and said, 'This is the hardest thing I've ever had to do, but I know one day you'll understand.'

All Lorna could understand was she'd chosen the other one and not her. Lorna wanted Katherine, but she wanted Katherine to be herself more than that. She knew she'd never be that in her chosen life.

As Katherine and her husband walked through the tunnel attached to the plane, she glanced out of the tiny window while they queued for a moment as passengers before them boarded.

Searching for a mint, Katherine felt through the pockets of her jacket. Passing the tickets to her husband so she could search better, she reached into one of the inner pockets and felt something sharp. She pulled out a necklace. She looked at it in her hand.

It was a peculiar piece of jewellery which is probably why she liked it so much in the first place. It had an invisible chain which was made from the type of plastic and several pieces of stone shaped like rectangles, which got smaller from the inside to the out. The stones were a mixture of blues, greens, purples and greys all mixed together. There were tiny blue beads threaded between the stones. It fastened with a silver clasp.

It had been Lorna's. Katherine had first seen it when she'd worn it the one time they'd met up. Lorna had wanted to give it to Katherine that day as she knew how much she liked the necklace, though it had a little financial value. Katherine wouldn't take it from her, so one afternoon after she'd been with Lorna in a restaurant and then later gone to meet her husband in another bar, Lorna had slipped it into Katherine's coat while she was ordering at the bar. Later that afternoon when Lorna knew Katherine would be sitting miserably in this pub without her, she sent a text message saying, 'Check your coat pocket'. When Katherine had excused herself to visit the ladies' room she reached into her pocket and found the necklace.

From that day she'd kept it and worn it out a number of times. Katherine's husband just thought it was another silly necklace she'd bought, but Katherine knew it was from Lorna and it had been hers.

'Your strange necklace darling.'

Katherine looked up at him. 'Yeah, I didn't know it was in here. I haven't seen it for some time actually.'

'It's so strange you know, throw it away and we'll get you a new, decent necklace in America.'

Katherine looked at him again and then at the necklace in her hand. She paused. It was as if her two lovers were standing in front of her and saying 'pick which one you want then. You can only have one, the other one you lose forever!'

'Yes OK, I guess you're right. A new necklace when we get to our new home. I'll just put it in here for now and get rid of it later.' Katherine, loosening the necklace, dropped it into a side pocket on her flight bag and then stood again to board. They were at the door.

'Your tickets please Sir.'

Katherine took one final glance from the small window, and for just a moment she disappeared into her thoughts as the tickets were checked. *He has my life, but you Lorna will always have my heart.*

MY BEST FRIEND'S HUSBAND
Susie Field

Hayley watched in dismay as her best friend Molly exchanged wedding vows with her handsome fiancé Rob. She was chief bridesmaid and should have been happy for her friend, yet she was torn apart with jealousy. When Rob had arrived on their social scene, Hayley had wanted him desperately, and had used every trick in the book to hook him. It had always worked in the past - one toss of her long blonde hair and the guys were smitten, but not Rob. He was tall and dark with a wicked sense of humour, and he had chosen Molly. Hayley watched her smiling up at Rob - she did look quite pretty - but after all it was her wedding day - all brides looked pretty on their wedding day. Her dress clung to her slim figure and her black curls danced around her bare shoulders. Rob's expression was one of total adoration - how she wished the wedding was over. She forced a smile and tried to ignore the stares of Rob's best man. He looked okay and obviously had the hots for her - but he wasn't Rob.

The reception was even worse. How could she bear to watch Molly and Rob dancing so closely - occasionally kissing. It was so unfair.

'Hi beautiful,' a deep voice broke into her thoughts.

Hayley turned around.

'How about a dance with the best man?' It was Mikey.

'Why not?' Hayley shrugged ungraciously.

Mikey held her closely as they swayed to the music. He looked quite nice she supposed - although he was a bit plastered. She didn't object when he bent his head to kiss her - he was an excellent kisser - might as well enjoy herself. She had hoped to make Rob jealous, but he hadn't really noticed. Even when she asked Rob for a dance it was quite obvious he couldn't wait to get back to Molly. Hayley turned her attention to Mikey.

'Would you like to come back to my place?' he slurred.

'Why not?' Hayley replied. 'I'll just say goodbye to Molly and Rob - wish them a good honeymoon.' That was something she did not want to think about. Rob in bed with Molly.

Hayley continued to see Mikey - he was quite good fun when he wasn't drunk - which wasn't often, but at least it kept her close to Rob. Twelve months had passed since the wedding, and Hayley flirted with

Rob at every opportunity but to no avail. When Molly announced she was pregnant, Hayley thought she was going to be sick. Rob was delighted at the prospect of becoming a father and as Molly's figure expanded rapidly, Hayley's clothes became more revealing - it still didn't work.

When Molly presented Rob with a beautiful daughter, he was over the moon. Hayley joined in his enthusiasm as she sat with Mikey in the wine bar.

'I'll go and see Molly tomorrow,' Hayley said pleasantly. 'I can't wait to see the baby,' she lied.

'Oh she's beautiful,' Rob answered dreamily. 'Just like Molly.'

Hayley turned away. They ordered more drinks and eventually Mikey was so drunk he could hardly stand.

'We'd better take him home,' Rob said anxiously. He'd also had a lot to drink and it was a struggle getting Mikey into the cab.

'I'll stay the night with him,' Hayley announced as they settled Mikey into bed. 'Make sure he's okay.'

'Good idea,' Rob replied. 'I'll ring for a cab.'

'Why don't you stay for a coffee?' Hayley asked. 'It might sober us both up a little.'

'Okay,' Rob replied easily.

Hayley wandered into Mikey's kitchen and unfastened two more buttons on her dress - maybe this was her chance.

'Here we are,' she said, sitting close to Rob and handing him a steaming mug of coffee.

They sat in silence for a while, and then she noticed Rob actually glancing at her legs in the tiny skirt - so he was human.

'What are you looking at?' she teased, moving closer - making sure her ample cleavage was on display.

'Nothing,' Rob replied nervously. 'Look, I'd better get going.'

'Don't go Rob,' Hayley said, wrapping her arms around his neck and kissing him on the lips.

'What about Mikey?' Rob asked suddenly.

'Don't worry about him. He's dead to the world,' Hayley laughed.

She kissed Rob again and he kissed her back. Hayley melted under his touch - it was better than she'd ever imagined - absolute magic. They were soon rolling naked on the floor and about to make love when Rob suddenly pulled away.

'What's the matter?' Hayley asked.

'What are we doing?' Rob replied as he ran his fingers through his thick hair and struggled into his clothes. 'Get dressed Hayley. How the hell did this happen?'

'It's what we've always wanted,' Hayley whispered, trying to pull him towards her.

'No it isn't, Hayley,' Rob was distraught. 'I have everything I want - Molly and the baby. I've never wanted anyone else.'

'You wanted me just now,' Hayley shrieked.

'It's the drink,' Rob replied - the tears stinging his eyes. How could he do this to Molly and the baby. 'We're both drunk - let's just forget it.'

'How convenient,' Hayley snapped. 'What if I don't want to forget it?'

'Nothing happened here, Hayley,' Rob was yelling.

'Nothing happened?' Hayley laughed viciously. 'We were naked on the floor - all over each other and you say nothing happened. I wonder if your precious Molly would call it nothing. I don't *think* so.'

'Please don't tell her,' Rob begged. 'Please Hayley. She'd be destroyed. I love her so much.'

'You should have thought about that before chasing me,' Hayley said bitterly.

'I didn't chase you.' Rob was already calling for a cab. 'Come on Hayley - you're supposed to be Molly's best friend.'

'And you're supposed to be her husband,' Hayley said sarcastically. 'I'm your best mate's girlfriend remember. Not a pretty picture. Poor Molly - she'll be devastated.

Rob could hardly remember the journey home. He ripped off his clothes and threw himself onto the bed. His gaze travelled to the tiny cradle - carefully prepared. What an idiot he'd been - he could lose everything he held so dear.

Hayley was furious. The feelings of rejection threatened to engulf her. How dare he treat her like this - arrogant b*****d. Well, she would show him. She couldn't wait to wipe the smug smile off Molly's face.

Rob woke early from a restless sleep and headed straight to the hospital. He was glad it was Saturday - he would be able to spend all day with Molly and the baby. Molly hadn't seen him enter the ward and the feelings of love overpowered him as he watched her feeding their baby. She glanced up and smiled as he hurried towards her.

'You look beautiful,' he said, kissing her tenderly.

'You look worse for wear,' she laughed. 'I bet you've got a hangover.'

'Just a bit,' he replied sheepishly.

'Where did you go?' Molly asked.

'Just out with Mikey and Hayley. Nothing special,' he answered quietly.

'Hayley's coming to see me later,' Molly smiled. 'I can't wait to show her the baby. I want her and Mikey to be godparents.'

'I don't think that's a good idea,' Rob said hesitantly.

'Why not?' Molly was amazed. 'They're our best friends.'

Rob swallowed hard and then he told her what had happened. Molly stared at him in disbelief as the tears fell down her cheeks.

'How could you?' she cried. 'I thought you loved me. With my best friend, when I've just had our baby. The two people I love most in the world. I can't bear it.'

'Please listen,' Rob begged, taking her hand. 'I didn't make love to her. I stopped. It must have been the drink.'

'I thought you were so special,' Molly said sadly. 'I've known Hayley since school and all the boys wanted her - never me. I thought you were different - but you're not.'

'I am, please believe me Molly. I've never wanted Hayley.'

'But she's always wanted you,' Molly replied, looking directly at him. 'Why did you have to tell me?'

'I wanted you to know the truth.' Rob took the baby from her arms and cradled her gently. 'I swear I did not make love to her. She was furious and threatened to tell you. Please don't let her come between us, Molly.'

'What about Mikey?' Molly asked.

'I don't think Hayley cares about Mikey,' Rob answered.

'I'm sure she doesn't,' Molly said bitterly. 'All Hayley cares about is herself.'

Rob handed the baby back to Molly and watched as she fed his child. He had ruined everything. 'Can you ever forgive me?' he pleaded.

'I suppose I'll have to forgive you. I love you,' Molly answered sadly. 'But I can't forgive Hayley. She knew exactly what she was doing and you were drunk. I'm still furious Rob - if you ever do anything like this again - we're finished.'

'You know I won't.' Rob was openly crying. 'I'll make it up to you Molly.'

Molly nodded. 'I want you to go now Rob,' she whispered. 'I need to think. I want to be ready for Hayley when she visits.'

Rob didn't want to leave but Molly insisted. He felt dreadful. 'I'll come back later,' he said. 'Is there anything you need?'

'All I ever needed, Rob, was you.'

Rob would never forget the sadness in her eyes.

Molly showered and washed her hair, applying her make-up carefully. She pulled a clean night-dress over her head and waited. Hayley looked absolutely stunning as she walked towards the bed carrying a small parcel for the baby.

'You look well,' Hayley announced - she hadn't expected her to look quite so good. 'I thought Rob would be here.'

'He's gone,' Molly replied - her voice was flat. 'I think he had a hangover.'

'I'm not surprised,' Hayley laughed. 'We had to put Mikey to bed. He was totally off his head.'

'Rob told me,' Molly replied, staring at her friend.

'What else did he tell you?' Hayley asked. She couldn't hide the triumph in her voice.

'Why did you do it?' Molly whispered. 'How could you come onto Rob like that?'

'Is that what he said?' Hayley laughed, as she tossed her blonde hair. 'He was all over me like a rash. I had to fight to stop him making love to me. I felt sorry for you.'

'I don't believe you,' Molly replied angrily. 'It was Rob who stopped and you know it. You've always wanted him just because he was mine. You could have anyone you wanted apart from Rob. You were jealous because he wanted me. I hate you.' Molly burst into tears just as the baby began to cry heartily. She reached across for the tiny child and held her to her breast.

Hayley watched her friend sorrowfully. She had been a good friend for many years - kind and sincere. No wonder Rob loved her so much.

'I'm sorry,' Hayley said suddenly. 'So very sorry Molly. You're right - I did want Rob and I was jealous because he never wanted me. I tried to take advantage because he was drunk, but he still didn't want me.'

'Get out,' Molly shouted. 'And take your present with you. I never want to see you again.'

Hayley ran from the ward. What had she done? She had lost her only true friend. She needed someone to talk to - Mikey - he would listen.

'I've got one hell of a headache,' Mikey moaned as Hayley walked into the kitchen. He'd just showered and was naked apart from a towel wrapped around his waist. 'What's the matter with you?'

Hayley burst into tears and sobbed uncontrollably. Mikey rushed towards her and guided her to the sofa. Between her sobs she told him everything.

'I bet you hate me too,' she cried, looking directly at him.

'I don't hate you Hayley,' Mikey sighed, kissing her forehead. 'I've always known you fancied Rob and never really wanted me. I hoped that in time you might change your mind. I couldn't believe my luck when you agreed to go out with me. I'd forgive you anything, Hayley. I love you - fool that I am. I wonder sometimes if you even like me.'

'Oh I do like you, Mikey,' Hayley replied, nestling her head against his bare chest. 'I suppose I never realised how much - until now.'

Mikey bent his head and kissed her.

'You always were a great kisser,' Hayley laughed, pulling him closer.

Mikey's hangover was soon forgotten.

Molly smiled at Rob as they strolled in the park. The weeks after the birth had been difficult for them both. Rob had been wonderful and she knew how bitterly he regretted what had happened with Hayley. He was a good husband and father.

'I saw Mikey the other day,' Rob said suddenly, as he steered the pram carefully across the muddy ground. 'He was with Hayley - they're engaged. Hayley said that she missed you Molly and hoped that some day you could be friends again.'

'I miss her too,' Molly replied thoughtfully. 'I hope she'll be very happy with Mikey - I really do. Perhaps I should give her a ring. Would you mind?'

'Of course not,' Rob answered. 'I must admit I miss Mikey - we've always been mates.'

'That's settled then.' Molly felt much better. 'I'll invite them round to supper to celebrate their engagement.'

'I love you,' Rob whispered, bending to kiss her tenderly.

'I know you do,' Molly laughed. 'And I love you, Rob.'

THE SEWING BOX
Merle Sadler

Cissie Harris was well-known and liked in the small community - she had long chestnut hair reaching almost to her waist, brown eyes and rosy dimpled cheeks.

The youngest daughter of the family, she had a brother, Charles and a sister, Annie, and was made much of with her sunny nature and ready smile.

Her parents, Henry and Sarah had kept a small grocery/general shop for many years, having regular customers who were regarded as friends. The shop was considered to be a hub for local families as there was little which could not be purchased at 'H W Turnbull - Grocery and General Store'. Cissie's father was a dapper little man, black hair brushed neatly back from a somewhat florid face and he always wore a freshly starched white apron. He liked to discuss day-to-day events with his customers, considering this geniality to be an important part of his business.

Her mother was small and quiet, preferring to stay in the background and generally keep herself busy in the shop, dusting and stocking shelves, as well as serving customers.

Cissie worked in a dress shop - winning over everyone with her friendly manner and ready smile.

She liked to make her own dresses and would study the latest fashions in 'Victoria Gowns' and adapt them to her own style. Being clever with her needle, she was always smartly attired.

Alfred Picken was tall and fair with grey eyes and a serious expression.

He was the oldest in the family, having two sisters, Florence and Edith, who looked up to him and regarded him with great respect. He, in turn, was always ready to listen to them and address any problems with grave consideration.

Alfred worked in a small family furniture business 'A Smith & Son - Makers of Fine Furniture'. The owner was an old friend of the Harris family and knowing him to be conscientious, took Alfred into the firm on leaving school.

Alfred worked diligently, anxious to learn and loved fashioning the wood into finished items of furniture under the watchful eye of Samuel, who had been in the business for many years and took pleasure in sharing his craftsmanship with this serious, likeable young lad.

In the spring of 1912, on a warm Sunday afternoon, there were the usual visitors to the park - the Brass Band Concert proving an attraction to young and old alike.

The band was made up of local musicians, the older members smart and erect of carriage kept a stern eye on the younger element, who, freshly scrubbed and hair neatly brushed, were apt to become restive unless under scrutiny.

It was here, then, on just such an afternoon, that Cissie and Alfred met for the first time.

Alfred thought that he had never met such a beguiling little creature, with her sweet smile and laughing eyes. He knew that he had to meet her again and when she agreed to be at the park at 3 o'clock the following Sunday, he could scarcely contain his delight.

And so began the love affair of Cissie and Alfred - a love affair which Alfred considered was surely meant to be, that on an ordinary Sunday, love was to come into his life - a love which he knew would last for as long as he should live.

On a perfect day in September, 1914, Cissie and Alfred were married in their local church - Cissie in a demure white dress, her long auburn tresses caught up in a shining coil and Alfred, tall and handsome in his best striped suit.

Friends had packed the little church to witness the marriage and their families looked on proudly as they made their vows 'until death do us part'.

Alfred gave much consideration as to what he would give Cissie for her birthday - her first birthday as his wife. Whilst busy in the workshop, he thought of a splendid gift - a wooden sewing box, which he would make for her in his spare time - a symbol of his love for her.

The sewing box gradually took shape, fashioned with love and care and dreams of their future together. With delicate precision, he carved flowers and intricate scrolls, entwined with trailing leaves and lovers' knots.

In the centre of the box he formed her initial 'C' in cherry wood, encased within a mosaic design.

He lined the box with rich brown velvet, cushioning it carefully into the lid.

Alfred gazed at his finished box and traced her initial lovingly with his finger, a fond smile playing on his lips as he envisaged her expression when she received the exquisite sewing box.

In 1915, Alfred received his papers to enlist in the army and prepared to say farewell to Cissie.

As he was ready to leave, Cissie joyfully told him that she was expecting their child and so he left for France, both proud but also a little fearful for Cissie, who would be without him by her side.

Cissie busied herself in their little house, keeping it bright and welcoming, longing for the war to be over when they would all be together.

A knock on the door one morning shattered all her dreams. A telegram from the War Office regretted to inform her that Private Alfred Picken had been killed in action in France.

Shortly afterwards, Cissie's daughter, Emma, was born. Emma, already with her father's features and a tuft of her mother's auburn hair.

As she cradled the baby in her arms, Cissie told her of the love which she and Alfred had shared and that, one day, the sewing box would be hers to cherish.

The baby stretched out tiny pink fingers as if to embrace the future, symbolised by the intricately carved sewing box, created with such love and promise by her father, Alfred.

TEENAGER IN LOVE
Johnny Wallman

The cold January air bit deeply as Marilyn wrapped her scarf tightly around her uncovered neck, fastened her coat tight and walked briskly towards the clothes shop where she worked. She had been employed there since leaving school some six months previous. Not the most exciting of jobs, but her father, knowing the owner, Mrs Chandler, gave Marilyn no say in the matter.

Marilyn was late again. She could tell by the scowl on the old woman's battered old face. She apologised before scuttling into the back room to make the tea. Marilyn found it amusing, especially as no one ever came into the shop.

'I have to go out for a little while, will you manage on your own?' asked Mrs Chandler, already donning her coat as she spoke.

Marilyn smiled. The old lady asked the same question, at the same time, every day. The young girl wondered where she went every day, imagining some sordid affair or meeting with a top-secret spy. Either way, it left her in charge of the shop and free to listen to the radio without the scorn of her elder. Marilyn watched the manageress cross the road and head towards the park. Once the old woman was out of sight, Marilyn took the radio and searched for her favourite station. Her favourite singer was Elvis, she hoped one of his songs would be played before the manageress returned. This was her only opportunity to listen to the songs she liked. Marilyn's father, a deeply religious man, disapproved of her taste in music. These two hours every day were her delve into the 1960s' world of freedom and love. Her father kept her on a tight leash. His temper frightened her and though he often lifted his hand in anger, it never connected to anything other than the now dented kitchen table. When Marilyn rarely wanted something, she would always ask through her mother.

Marilyn had an older brother who seemed to be allowed to do what he wanted, while she spent most of her time in the house helping her mother. She had few friends and none that ever came to the house. She resented her father a little for making the house so unwelcoming. Her mother said little, serving as the obedient housewife and mother. Marilyn's room was decorated with 1920s' flowered wallpaper and touched up every few years with a coat of cream emulsion. The only reference to the 1960s' revolution was a small postcard picture of Elvis pinned to the mirror on the dressing table. She had once dared to display a large poster of James Dean but her father considered him obscene and demanded its removal. In fact the swinging sixties had bypassed Marilyn's house completely. At school she had her admirers, her long light brown hair and deep blue eyes sending many of the boys into lovestruck obsessions. She had developed earlier than many of her girlfriends, making her even more of an attraction.

Her father, however, refused her requests to attend the evening youth club leaving her completely unobtainable. The boys soon lost interest.

Marilyn often wondered why she was kept on in the shop, hardly anybody ever came in, and if they did they almost always wanted the old woman to serve them. It seemed her job was to make tea and cover for two hours while the owner disappeared on her secret mission. Marilyn turned the radio louder. Looking through the front window, watching the world go by, she sang the words of the Everlys and Del Shannon. There had never been dreams of being a world-class ballerina or an intentionally acclaimed actress, just a hope of little more than her peers had settled for in this stifling, self-enforced ghetto.

It was just as she hit the high note of 'Runaway' that the shop door opened. Her hands still raised, and in mid-note, Marilyn smiled, attempting to hide her embarrassment. 'Hello, can I help you?' she asked.

'I hope so,' came the reply.

Marilyn looked at the figure as it drew closer to the counter. He was beautiful.

'I am looking for a nice scarf for my mother, it is her birthday,' he said.

Marilyn leaned below the counter and turned off the radio, pulling out the scarf drawer without looking away.

'We are new to the area, not long since arrived from Ireland. My name is Michael, and yours?' He held his hand out.

Marilyn, unsure whether to shake or place the scarves, chose to do the former.

They talked for an age. Marilyn had never really spoken to a man before. She struggled to concentrate on his words as all kinds of alien thoughts ran through her head. As he talked she watched his mouth, his lips close together and for the first time ever, she wanted to kiss someone. She felt the butterflies rise within her young heart. She could not stop her heart racing as Marilyn became hypnotised by Michael's pale blue eyes and golden hair. She knew she was stupid and that this was reserved for the movies, but this was love at first sight. She wanted this moment to last forever.

As the manageress returned, Michael politely thanked Marilyn for the helpful service and left the shop. Marilyn's eyes never left his aura as he walked from the shop, feeling his presence long after he had departed. It was not until a few moments later that she noticed he had forgotten the scarf. She picked it up and ran to the door but he was nowhere to be seen. The old woman watched her suspiciously. Marilyn knew that any transgression would be reported to her father.

'Who was that?' asked the old woman.

'He just came in to buy a scarf for his mother's birthday,' replied Marilyn, desperately trying to hide her excitement. She said nothing about how he had spent the best part of an hour chatting, that he was five years older than her, and most damaging, how he had asked her to the local disco on Saturday night.

Marilyn felt sure he would return the following day and hoped that the manageress would not cancel her daily disappearing act.

Arriving early the next morning, Marilyn had thought of nothing else but Michael all night. He must have been watching the shop, waiting for the old woman to leave, because as she crossed the road to the park, he entered the shop. Again they talked, this time for the two hours the old woman was away. He told her about his now discarded life in Ireland, his family and his hopes for the future.

'No, no, no, you are not going to any disco,' shouted her father.

Marilyn begged, explaining that she never went out, that she would be with friends and would be home well before midnight. The discussion was not a debate of equals. For every calculated, reasoned point made my Marilyn, there was a louder *no* from her father.

It was her mother that finally persuaded him to acquiesce. Marilyn never discovered what her mother had said to change his mind. She took that to her deathbed, along with the unfair guilt, blaming herself for the consequences of that decision.

Marilyn spent nearly the whole day brushing her hair in readiness. Nothing in her wardrobe remotely resembled anything as glamorous as the dresses of the Paris catwalk, but not even a dowdy dress would stop her now. Her father, a seasoned poor loser, stared silently at the blank wall. Her mother requested the customary twirl and gave Marilyn a secret wink.

Michael met her at the entrance to the small club and after paying her entrance fee, took her arm escorting her into the building. Marilyn's smile entered minutes before she did. The bright lights and the loud tunes dazzled her as she watched the crowd on the dance floor with an awe of wonderment. Michael led her to the dance floor just as Elvis asked if they were 'Lonesome Tonight'.

'I'm not,' she whispered to herself.

Michael leaned down and their lips touched. This was her first ever kiss and she felt the electricity through her body. He opened his mouth and she followed his lead. Her mother, knowing her daughter's genuine beauty, had told Marilyn that one day she would meet the right man, that she would just know it. As they hugged she felt warm and loved for the first time, she remembered her mother's words. Michael was the one.

They left the disco once Elvis had completed his song. The cold air bit sharply but Marilyn dismissed it. This was her chance to be alone with Michael and a freezing wind wasn't going to stop her. Hand in hand they walked towards the park, passing the shop as they did so.

'I still haven't collected that scarf,' Michael said.

They both laughed as they reached the closed park gates.

'Come on, let's climb over,' he said. Michael held Marilyn's arm as she clumsily negotiated the iron gate. The two laughed as he chased her between the trees, they played on the children's slide and swings. They kissed, played on the roundabout, then kissed some more. Both fell to the sodden grass, turned on their backs and gazed at the bright stars and full moon. Marilyn looked for a sign in a falling star, but none were forthcoming. Instead she turned to her side, her lips again meeting Michael's. She had fallen in love with Michael and knew that he had fallen for her.

The park was so quiet, the only sound was her heart beating. She could see the lights of the houses on the hill as her mind drifted to a future Michael. She held him tight. A huge oak tree hid the circling moon for a few minutes, throwing their small area of paradise into total darkness.

Neither spoke. As the church clock chimed at midnight, the two lay on the cold, icy grass, his trousers thrown into a nearby bush, her dress crumpled and raised. They kissed once again and smiled, their final kiss. They would never see each other again.

Michael opened the door to see two police officers. His mother led them into the living room, where they politely declined both a seat and a cup of tea.

'I am arresting you for performing unlawful, carnal knowledge.'

Michael walked quietly, turning only once to see the tears his mother now shed.

Two weeks later, Michael was back in Ireland. The thoughts of Marilyn taking considerably longer to erase.

Every part of Marilyn's body ached. She looked around the beds in the sterile nursing home. She had been admitted the minute she had started 'showing'. Her parents had told the neighbours she had found a job in London. She had signed all sorts of forms while half asleep, but suddenly it dawned on her exactly what those forms were. Her father had visited just twice, bringing various documents. Not once did he look her in the eye. She no longer felt frightened, but still very alone.

Marilyn felt no guilt. She had been, and still was, in love. She thought of Michael often, although his name was never mentioned but for that one occasion, several months before, as with all her dilemmas, Marilyn had first told her mother her period was late, very late. Her mother, not knowing what to do, demanded she told her father. Of course he flew into a blind rage.

Marilyn watched the nurse walk towards the exit, her high heels clicking on the polished floor. With each step a loud click, with each click she felt a sharp pain right through her broken heart. She battled to focus through the tears as the nurse carried her baby out of the ward and out of her life.

MEETING OF MINDS
Lynda O'Neill

Andrew Carnegie was a power-crazy businessman but he did do something that justified his stay on the planet; splashed the cash on building public libraries. Where else can you get an education, great literature and a one-way ticket to another world?

I'm a librarian, and I think it's the best job in the world. We get a bad press: tight-arsed frumps who hiss 'Quiet please'? Forget it. I work with Mary who's into S&M once she sheds the A-line skirt and high-necked blouse. Not to mention John, who swears like a navvy once customers are out of earshot. Every Monday he tells me about Saturday's visit to a gay club with a special room downstairs where people do things that make me want to say 'Less information *please*'. The head librarian, Patricia (never Trish to her face), is the exception that proves the rule. She's got a tic, a fixation with navy blue polyester and a mouth like a Pekinese's arse.

Why is it so great? Books. The smell of new ones - too few, thanks to a safeseat councillor with a double-barrelled name who sees no votes in raising the book grant. There's the chance of getting my head into a thick novel during coffee break and escaping from my problems - you can't be mithering about your mother or the alcoholic womaniser at home with your head in *War and Peace*. 'Back to the desk, please!' snorts Trish when I'm three pages into the latest Margaret Atwood.

And people. It's the ideal way to clock them and their choice of books. I frown over the obsolete computer system that's always crashing, or pile up returned books with an impassive face as I eavesdrop. Librarians rarely comment on books borrowed; it's just not done, a bit like a doctor whispering, 'Appalling irritable bowel, poor girl', to the person your hostess introduces to him as you move away.

I've been here ten years, and one or two, old regulars mostly, I know by name. There's Mrs Vaughan, a widow half demented with loneliness who comes in twice a week for a Mills & Boon. I ask after the children and grandchildren she rarely sees. I get the feeling I'm the only person she'll speak to that day. We exchange Christmas cards; Dickensian carriage scene with glitter from her, something with a robin from the box I keep for aunties from me.

There's Mr Buxton and Mr Ayling, who raise their hats and call me 'Miss' with a lovely smile. They come in to get out from under their wives' feet and loiter by 'Railway' or 'Military History'. And we get the odd vagrant stinking of p**s who comes in to read the newspapers and get warm, though I have to hoick these out on Trisha's instructions if they get too pungent near the radiators.

You wouldn't believe some of the conversations I hear as I stack the shelves.

'How can I contact a contract killer?' whispered by Mrs Twinset and Pearls to a louche man who always takes out murder stories or, once, an explicit account of the previous night's threesome from a pale, knackered student by the Plays Section.

'Performing Arts student with a fevered imagination,' snorts Mary over Nescafe and a Harvest Crunch later, though I'd felt it had the ring of truth.

We're supposed to make sure nothing's been left in books when they return, but I'm one of the few who actually does. Otherwise it's an opportunity lost to spy on people's lives: railway tickets (what sort of day did they have - illicit meetings, museum trips, duty visit to a relative?) Postcards - was the second honeymoon in Venice a success or did they do nothing but argue? Were the kids a nightmare on that Majorcan fortnight? And the *letters*. Dull ones to Mum that don't tell her what she really wants to know, long abusive ones in capital letters with no signature, illiterate but tender love letters, those of the 'What I intend to do to you' variety that bring a flush to my cheeks and give me ideas. Phone bills with large sums circled (teenager in the family?), hotel bills for a weekend away, once a condom (in its wrapper, thank God) marking the place in *Sense and Sensibility*.

I always have a quick squint through to see if anything's been written in the margins. 'Palpable nonsense', or 'Research full of holes. See Antonia Fraser's book on the subject . . .' Sometimes I see 'Mrs so-and-so at 12 Railway Road is a whore. Ring her on . . .' If they're like this I stick a label over the writing. If not, I leave it to entertain someone else.

About two years ago there seemed to be a rash of these little notations in the collections of diary entries and biographies. Things like 'What did his father do to deserve this book?' with the reply, 'Don't agree. Writes like an angel . . .' And they didn't just appear in the weighty ones; Noel Coward's had a sprinkling of 'Self-obsessed old fart' and 'Sure. But don't you just *love* the way he writes about his mum and how she enjoyed the weekend parties as Goldenhurst? And he's so funny when he says that despite what Gertie says she *wasn't* chewing kippers in the gutter as a child'.

These people weren't above taking out trashy showbiz ones by cheesy old actors who trot out the 'Well, they seemed to like me well enough in Kidderminster' routine or ghosted, glossed-over life stories of actresses with three facelifts and kids who hadn't spoken to them in twenty years.

The correspondents obviously had a lot in common. I decided to check who'd returned them next time I flipped through one before stacking it on the trolley.

The one with the angular black scrawl was James Fisher. I'd often seen him; fortyish, cord trousers, scuffed casual shoes (though not, thank God, with that crimped seam all round - Cornish pasty shoes, Mary calls them). His curly black hair needed styling but the suede jacket looked expensive, if worn.

The turquoise italics belonged to Nina Mendellsohn. *What a beautiful name*, I thought, and wished I knew her, because her comments betrayed a gentle, subversive humour.

The notes increased. I worried that another librarian would see them and put labels on them or take the book out of circulation. I read the message and was alert for their visits, which were never predictable, apart from James calling in after work on Wednesdays. I knew nothing of these people apart from their addresses and the other books they borrowed apart from biographies. Thrillers and science fiction for James, contemporary novels and layman's books on psychology for Nina, though not so tame you could call them self-help.

Their visits grew more frequent and one day I realised who Nina was. She had one of those faces that isn't beautiful but so striking you can't keep your eyes off it, with a Roman nose that only added to its character. Her clothes were arty-farty - a look I've tried but with less success - and her black boots could have used a polish, but she had a smile she didn't keep for special occasions.

I busied myself at the PC and watched her pick books off the shelves. She looked into half a dozen in quick succession. Then she smiled, shut a fat biography of Philip Larkin and brought it back to the desk. What was written in it, I wondered, wishing I could look as I stamped it.

A week later as I pressed buttons on the computer, James slapped three books on the desk. He stood sideways as he looked through the Larkin biography Nina had returned the previous day. He had a pleasing Heathcliff quality. He read a chunk of the book and leafed through, stopping to read something that provoked a can't-help-it grin.

These two were *made* for each other. It was time they met and I was going to make it happen. It called for a creative approach. I went home, posted the idea to my subconscious and hoped an idea would plop through its letterbox.

A week later a plan surfaced. Instead of going out for a walk at lunchtime - which usually amounted to a series of wistful sighs at clothes I couldn't afford in Monsoon - I decided to take a stack of the latest biographies to the work room and flip through them to keep up with the messages.

As usual they were pertinent, literate, amusing. 'Too much made of his sexual proclivities', or 'Sure. But what a prize s**t!' or 'Time the publisher made sure the writer did more than regurgitate cuttings when they charge twenty quid for a biog', with the reply, 'Yeah. Money for old rope'.

In three books, to maximise the chance of her seeing it - an edition of James Lees-Milne's diaries from the sixties, a weighty Claire Tomalin biography and Blake Morrison's latest - I forged James' hand; 'I'll be here on Wednesday at 6pm. I'm tall with dark hair. Shall we meet?' *Nothing too pushy,* I thought; *she can take it or leave it.*

She took it. I was thrilled to see them arrive five minutes apart and stand by the shelf where it had all started. She eyed all the men in the vicinity. Her face fell at a couple of guys she saw - the knackered student, ironically, and one of my retired regulars in a shortie raincoat - but then she saw James. She looked away and busied herself in a book. He, of course, was unaware of what I'd written.

She continued to engross herself in books, then looked sideways at him. She pointed to a comment I'd written and said something. He looked puzzled for a moment, then bemused. The other people moved away and they talked in a way that was alternately bashful and excited. I could hardly contain myself but managed to wear my professional face as I stamped *Uncle Tungsten* for him and something by Joan Wyndham for her.

After this I saw them separately but never together. The written comments had dried up. Oh well, I'd done my best. About a year ago I noticed Nina was pregnant.

Last week I had a run-in with Trish over the stack of fines letters I hadn't had time to do. The words 'verbal warning' reared their ugly head and I made the mistake of shrugging my shoulders and walking away, managing somehow to stop myself saying, 'Gimme a break, can't you . . .' She's been trying to find something to pin on me for years, ever since an office party when I photocopied my buttocks after three glasses of mulled wine. But I soon cheered up when James and Nina came in together. James had a baby strapped to his chest. They were talking and smiling.

I wondered if they'd ever worked out my part in it. Could have been anyone, couldn't it?

Forgery's a criminal offence. Difficult to prove, though.

Now you see why it's the best job in the world.

SMOTHER LOVE
Joyce Walker

'The trouble with Mother,' Alan said, 'is that she hasn't learnt to let go. I half expect her to phone me every morning to make sure I've changed my underwear and put a clean hankie in my pocket, or to remind me to go to the loo before I go to class.'

It would have been funny if it hadn't been too close to the truth.

To Edith Parker, Alan had been the only good thing to come out of a disastrous marriage and after his father left home, she smothered him. Her possessiveness had been fine when he was younger, for there was nothing he couldn't persuade her to do for him. When, however, he grew into his teens and started to take an interest in the opposite sex, life had become impossible.

She managed to find a way of coming between him and any girl he took a liking to. That was why he'd worked so hard to get to university. He had to escape so he could have a life of his own. It was also why he didn't tell her about Jade.

Jade was as beautiful as her name and he'd fallen in love with her almost from the first time he'd seen her in the college book shop where she worked. Now, after a year of going out together, they'd set up home.

They might have managed to live happily ever after without Edith ever knowing if Alan hadn't contracted a virus that almost killed him.

The two women met for the first time in a visitors' waiting room outside the intensive care unit. Edith, distraught because her son was lying unconscious and upset because the news had been given to her by this stranger who had taken her place in his affections, blamed Jade for everything that had happened to him.

'This would never have happened if he'd been living at home with me. I don't suppose you've been feeding him properly.'

'We live well enough,' Jade replied, too tired to quarrel with her. 'We both work, so we don't starve.'

'He works?' Edith asked.

'Just a part-time in a pub. It helps to pay the rent.'

'No wonder he's ill, he can't work and study. He's worn himself out, just so that the two of you can play house. Well, I'll tell you one thing my girl, as soon as he's well enough to leave here he's coming home with me and he's not coming back till he's 101% fit.'

The only thing that the two of them seemed to have in common was that they both wanted him to get well again.

They would take it in turns to sit by his bedside and make grudging promises to inform the other of any change.

When he regained consciousness five days later it was Jade who was keeping vigil while Edith slept in the small rest room. His head hurt, but he managed to say her name and it was a relief to be recognised and to be able to answer his where, why and how long.

'I'd better go and tell your mother you're awake, she'll want to come and talk to you.'

If only his head had been clearer he might have told her he wasn't up to his mother's fussing, but by the time the 'Jade, stay', had passed from his mind to his lips, she'd already left.

It took him 3 weeks to regain enough strength to be allowed home and during that time his mother seemed always to be there. Her constant pressure to try and make him return to the family home to convalesce was getting him down.

'I'm behind with classes already,' he protested.

'I'm sure your lecturers would give you some work to take back with you if you asked them to. Anyway the doctors say you need to rest away from the pressures of university life, so returning to classes too soon is definitely not the answer. If you stay here with that . . . that girl, you'll be back in here again within days and next time you might not be so lucky.'

He finally agreed that at least part of what she said might be true.

'Two weeks,' he said. 'I'll come home for two weeks, but that's all.'

Perhaps, thought Edith, *two weeks would be long enough to get that silly young woman out of his head.*

On the day Alan left hospital, Edith saw the flat he shared with Jade for the first time. It was small but surprisingly well cared for. She had gone inside with him to collect a few things for him to take back and as she looked about her, he misread her expression completely.

'Not much of a place, is it? But it'll pass for home until I can get a decent job and we can afford somewhere better.' After a pause he added, 'Look, I have to say goodbye to Jade, why don't you make yourself a cup of coffee or something. I'll meet you at the car in about an hour.'

The book shop was quiet at that time of day and Jade stopped talking to her workmate and smiled at him across the counter in much the same way as she had on the first day he walked in there.

'Well, hello,' she said, 'how are you feeling?'

He was more shaky than he cared to admit, so he just said OK before asking if she could take an early lunch break and walk him back to the car.

'All right,' she replied, 'there's something I want to tell you anyway. I haven't had chance with your mother breathing down our necks the whole time.'

Absorbed in serious conversation, they seemed totally unaware of Edith's presence. Stopping a few yards away from her they turned to face each other.

She watched through the car mirror as Jade put her arms round Alan's waist while he cupped her face in his hands and gently wiped away a tear with his thumb.

As the love scene played out before her, she felt like an intruder, but she realised she was no longer jealous.

Memories of earlier, happy times with Alan's father flooded back. As her son brought his lips down on Jade's in a goodbye kiss and she reached up and touched his pale cheek telling him to get well and come back to her, she realised that if she didn't make some sort of compromise she'd lose him completely.

When he finally got into the passenger seat beside her, she said, 'I thought you might like to ask Jade to visit us on Sunday. I think it's time we got to know each other, don't you?'

It was the first time he'd heard her call her by name, and he smiled broadly. 'I'm so glad you said that because I've already invited her. After all, she is going to be the mother of your grandchild.'

FIRST IMPRESSIONS
Margaret Webster

Vicki was already outside the beauty shop when Claire arrived.

'There's a 3 for 2 offer; and my face is crying out for tea-tree oil,' Vicki gushed, pulling her inside. 'But you look as if you're in need of a full facial - what's up?'

'Jake,' Claire answered, raising an eyebrow. 'He has planned a 'girlfriend meets his parents' evening. I'm just not sure I'm ready for this. But you know how persuasive Jake can be,' she grimaced.

'So, when is this date with destiny?' Vicki asked, rummaging in her purse for change.

'This Saturday.' Claire leant heavily on the counter. 'You've been through this Vick, and survived. You've got to help me out,' Claire pleaded. 'How is it done?'

Vicki steered Claire towards the aromatherapy section. 'First rule - relax. A good long soak in your favourite bubble bath with a few scented candles works wonders.' She ran her hand along the row of oils. 'And secondly - act naturally, there is no need to put on a performance. Just be yourself.'

Claire peered at herself in the large mirror behind the shelves. 'Myself. That's what worries me; I'm no good at meeting new people. What do I say?'

'Well, don't steal all the conversation and talk too much!' Vicki laughed and touched her mouth. 'That's *my* problem. And keep off taboo subjects - no politics, religion, s . . .'

Claire spluttered helplessly and left the shop.

'Soaps!' Vicki finished indignantly once outside on the path. 'If you back the wrong horse, Jake will never forgive you. Believe me! Mark should have let me know that there was a fatal distinction between a Street and a Close!' she rolled her eyes meaningfully. 'No searching questions either,' Vicki wagged her finger. 'Let Jake take the lead, after all he knows both sides.'

'And it was his idea,' Claire sighed. 'I don't really think soaps will be an issue - it's more likely to be medical dramas.'

'Oh yes. The family are all doctors aren't they? Jake must be a bit of a disappointment, being into media studies.'

Claire prickled. 'They can think what they like, he isn't a disappointment to me.' She stopped walking. 'But how will I shape up? I'm not really into dinner parties. I bet they have different cutlery for each course; dessert forks and goodness knows what.'

Vicki made an abrupt left turn into a book shop. 'If you're that worried then I'm sure we can find you something on the lines of *Table Etiquette for Beginners* in here,' she joked.

Claire held her back. 'I know, I'm being stupid! Jake mentioned something about pasta - salad - that sort of thing. A simple meal he said - nothing elaborate.'

'So, the scariest things on the table will be the salad servers,' Vicki reproached her. 'Or possibly a rampant pepper mill!'

Claire began to feel much better about the whole thing, and fell into a daydream about Jake's mild obsession with parmesan cheese. Until she passed the supermarket window. 'Wine!' she said, closing her eyes. 'I only drink sweet white wine and Jake likes a full-bodied red, it's what he drinks all the time.'

'Don't panic,' Vicki said reassuringly. 'You don't *have* to drink. It might give a good first impression.'

'You're right. If I drink, I might make a mess of things and give away some dreadful secrets.'

Vicki linked her arm. 'I thought I knew all your secrets. Are you holding out on me? Is there something Jake wouldn't want discussed over the fettuccini?'

They both laughed and knocked against a lady wheeling a shopping trolley. She turned and tutting loudly, gave them a disapproving 'act your age' look.

'What do you think I should wear?' Claire asked, sobering up. 'Most of my clothes are fairly casual these days, do you think casual is the right thing?'

Vicki shook her head. 'What you need for this 'meet the relatives' night is a new dress.'

'My budget won't stretch very far, is it necessary?'

'Who cares! It will give you the boost of confidence you need.'

Vicki was always quick to find an excuse to buy something new. A trip to the cinema often gave her just cause for another pair of shoes - though who would notice them in the dark puzzled Claire.

Claire finally succumbed to temptation when she noticed a sale at her favourite shop. They happily rifled through the racks of dresses and Claire held up a vivid red dress with a plunging neckline.

'What do you think?' she asked furtively. 'Is it a bit short?'

'It's certainly a bit short on fabric!' Vicki exclaimed. 'You are so lucky to be a size 10.' She pressed hard on her hips. 'It almost makes me want to give up chocolate.'

'I wouldn't look right in it would I?' Claire faltered.

'You would look fabulous in it. But not on this occasion.' Vicki took it and put it back on the rail. 'What we are looking for is sophistication.' She spun the carousel and landed on a midnight blue calf-length dress with a neat little slit up the side. 'Now here is the answer.'

It made Claire look taller. Height was definitely going to be an advantage and Vicki just happened to have a pair of shoes that would match.

Claire swung the bag defiantly. 'Now we need a coffee,' she chirped.

With two lattes and a Danish pastry between them, Vicki and Claire felt that they had made the most of their morning together. But Saturday evening still nagged away at Claire.

'Jake wants everyone to be on first name terms. No 'Mr and Mrs'. What do you think?' Claire asked anxiously. 'I don't want to appear stand-offish but is it not a bit too familiar the first time we meet? I wish I knew how *she* felt.'

'I agree with Jake. It's friendlier and it puts everyone at ease so she may expect it. It breaks down the barriers between the generations,' Vicki interlocked her fingers with their fashionably tattooed nails. 'I'm all for bridging the generation gap.' She leant forward. 'Anyway,' she whispered conspiratorially. 'It could be 'Mum and Dad' one day. What do you think of that?'

Claire took a deep breath and shook her head. 'One set of parents is enough for anyone.'

Vicki chuckled, 'I know what you mean.'

Claire suddenly looked worried. 'Do you think that's what is on Jake's mind? He can't - he's only in his first year of university. He's never spoken about 'long term' plans.'

'No, no,' Vicki soothed. 'Ignore my insane ramblings. As you say, he is only 19. He just wants to show you off, to prove he has a good taste in women.'

Claire nodded. 'I want this to go well.' She smiled, 'I suppose I want to be accepted. I have always been so proud of Jake. I want him to be proud of me.'

'He will be.' Vicki touched her hand. 'You're the best person I know, and the very best mum Jake could ever have. His girlfriend will love you!'

DÉJÀ VU
Terence Leslie

'I hope you are not going to become too obsessed with your family history,' Carol commented as she and Gilbert drove west out of Dublin.

'But, darling, one of the reasons for coming to Ireland was to trace my Irish roots,' he replied.

For over ten years Gilbert Michaels had been researching his ancestry. Many hours of pouring over family documents, parish registers and other genealogical material had led him to the discovery that he was probably descended from a certain Gilbert FitzMichael, a Normal knight who had taken part in the invasion of Ireland in the 12th century. As a reward for his exploits in that conquest, FitzMichael had been granted lands in the County of Dunrea, built a castle at Michaeltown and taken the title Earl of Dunrea. According to tradition his body was interred at the abbey of St Kieran at Ballydunrea a few miles outside Michaeltown.

'Listen, Carol, once I have satisfied myself about Gilbert FitzMichael then we can do whatever you want,' Gilbert said.

'Does that mean exercising your credit card?' Carol mocked.

'To a certain extent,' he replied.

'How far are the nearest beaches from Michaeltown?' she asked.

'Oh, about twenty miles. I hear they are very fine,' Gilbert said.

'Good, let's hope the weather is warm and sunny so that I can top up my tan.'

It was late afternoon when they arrived in Michaeltown. They had reservations at the aptly named Gilbert Hotel. After a refreshing shower they enjoyed a leisurely dinner with wine.

'I thought they might have given us Irish stew,' Carol smirked.

'Oh, it might have been worse. They could have given us 'Colcannon',' Gilbert said.

'What on Earth is that?' Carol exclaimed.

'A bit like bubble and squeak. Just potatoes and cabbage.'

In contrast their meal was a delight. A warming carrot and coriander soup, a prime roast of beef with assorted vegetables and Black Forest gateau to finish. Gilbert chose a bottle of Claret and later they relaxed with Irish coffee.

Carol complained of tiredness and went off to bed whilst Gilbert ordered a Jameson whiskey and a small jug of water. Taking a seat in the lounge bar he had just settled down when the door opened and a beautiful girl entered accompanied by a much older couple, presumably her parents. She had jet black hair and the bluest eyes he had ever seen. When she smiled her teeth showed small, even and brilliantly white. The three sat down at a table close to Gilbert and in a musical brogue the girl asked,

'What yer havin'?'

The older woman asked for a dry white wine whilst the man requested a whiskey and water.

Once the drinks were served the old couple raised their glasses and voiced, 'Happy birthday, Fiunella.'

Then the old woman took a package from her handbag and handed it to the girl. Fiunella opened it to reveal a necklace case and inside a gold chain bearing a Celtic cross. Her eyes widened with delight.

'Oh, thank you, Mammy and Dadda.'

A tear glistened in the corner of her eye, and getting up from her seat she went to her parents and kissed them.

A waiter appeared from the direction of the restaurant and announced that their table was ready so, finishing their drinks, they went in to dinner leaving Gilbert to reflect dreamily on the beautiful Fiunella.

Next morning, over breakfast, Gilbert expressed a wish to visit the local library and tourist information centre in order to find out more about his ancestor, Gilbert FitzMichael.

'In that case you had better hand over your credit card and I'll indulge in a little retail therapy. There's a nice woollen mill just outside town,' Carol answered, 'If I take the car I can drop you off, OK?'

'That's fine,' Gilbert smiled, 'So long as you don't clean me out.'

Once inside the library Gilbert went over to the enquiry desk and finding no one behind it gave the bell a smart smack with the palm of his hand. An office door opened and a familiar face appeared. It was Fiunella.

'Can I help you?' she asked in her musical brogue.

'Oh, I do hope so,' Gilbert replied with a smile. 'I am looking for some information on an ancestor of mine. He was Gilbert FitzMichael who came to Ireland in the 12th century. I understand he was the Earl of Dunrea and built a castle here.'

Fiunella's eyes widened and she flashed her white teeth.

'Well, this is a coincidence. My name is Fiunella FitzMichael and he is also my ancestor. We have a series of volumes entitled 'The FitzMichael Papers' on our shelves. Would you like to look through them?'

'Oh, yes. That would be great,' Gilbert replied.

'OK then. Whilst I am getting out the books would you please fill in one of these forms with your name and address? These books are quite valuable and disreputable dealers have been known to steal copies.' She handed him one from a nearby pile and then went off to get the volumes.

Soon she was back with an armful of slightly worn leather bound books.

'The reading room is this way, if you will follow me,' Fiunella said.

They crossed the reception area to a big brown door clearly marked. Inside were two rows of wooden tables with chairs set at either side. As Fiunella laid down the books Gilbert said, 'Let me introduce myself. My name is Gilbert Michaels. Somewhere along the line my ancestors seem to have dropped the Fitz and added the 's'.'

'Perhaps your branch of the family got into trouble and had to flee from Ireland?' Fiunella suggested.

'Maybe so,' Gilbert replied, 'would it be possible for us to meet up later to discuss our family trees? Have you done any research on the FitzMichaels?'

'Oh, yes. My branch of the family are descended from one of Gilbert FitzMichael's sons, Edmund FitzMichael. Perhaps he is your ancestor too. I don't have the time right now to talk at length but tomorrow is my day off. Maybe we could meet up?'

Gilbert's heart skipped a beat. What a wonderful opportunity to be alone with such a beautiful girl and a distant relative possibly.

'I was thinking of taking a ride out to Ballydunrea Abbey to look at Gilbert's tomb. Would you like to come with me? We could talk on the way.'

Fiunella was already warming to this tall, dark and handsome man with the slightly satanic appearance so she said, 'That would be nice. Where shall we meet?'

'I'll pick you up outside here at 10.30am tomorrow if that's OK? Maybe we could have lunch somewhere.'

That evening over dinner Gilbert told Carol of his intention to visit Ballydunrea Abbey to see the tomb of Gilbert FitzMichael.

'Do you want to come with me?' he asked casually.

'No, darling, it's not my scene. They have a lovely leisure centre here in the hotel. I fancy a nice swim and relaxing in the jacuzzi. You go and do your thing.'

Gilbert smiled. He didn't mention the fact that he was to be accompanied by Fiunella.

'That's OK, my dear. I should be back in good time for dinner. In fact I might have a swim myself before we eat.'

After their meal they went along to an evening of Irish dancing in the hotel ballroom. Gilbert drooled over the pretty Irish girls and whispered to Carol, 'Do you think I could take one of those home as a souvenir?'

Carol turned to him with a mocking smile and whispered back, 'Not unless you can get me Ronan Keating from Boyzone.'

Fiunella was waiting as he pulled up outside the library. She was wearing a summer dress with a flowery pattern which accentuated her trim figure. He felt strangely attracted to her and entertained the fanciful thought that they had met once before in a former life. She wished him a cheery good morning as she climbed into the car and soon they were heading out into the Irish countryside.

'So now. Tell me what you know about our common ancestor,' Gilbert asked.

'Well, he came over to Ireland in 1169 in an invading force under the leadership of Richard de Clare who was better known as Strongbow.'

'Did his family make cider?'

'No,' she giggled. 'The cider company just borrowed the name.'

'Oh,' he sighed in mock disappointment.

Fiunella went on, 'Because of his exploits during the conquest he was given lands in Dunrea and built the castle at Michaeltown. He married Fiunella O'Brian, the daughter of Conel O'Brian, a local chieftain. They had four sons, Gilbert, Michael, Nicholas and Edmund, from whom I am said to be descended. There were two daughters, Katherine and Joanna.'

'So we are named after the happy couple,' Gilbert commented.

'Yes, strange isn't it that we should meet up?' Fiunella added.

'Déjà vu?' he queried.

'Maybe,' she replied.

The Abbey was situated in meadow land on the banks of the River Rea. The skyline was dominated by a conical tower standing at the corner of the main building partly restored. This was now used as a place of worship. Within these confines the tomb of Gilbert FitzMichael was located in a small side chapel. The tomb was of black marble and surmounted with the effigies of a knight and his lady. Behind this a stained glass window showed the pair. He was wearing a helm, surcoat and armour whilst she was dressed in a long gown of red bodice and gold skirt. A blue cloak covered her shoulders. Her hair was long, auburn and a green band embroidered in gold encircled her head. A framed inscription mounted on the wall read, 'The tomb of Gilbert FitzMichael and his wife Fiunella Earl and Countess of Dunrea.'

Alongside were some notes relating to the couple. Gilbert was said to have been born in 1145, the son of Michael FitzRichard, the constable of Downchester Castle in Downshire, England. The date of his death was given as 1196 with the comment, 'Killed whilst hunting near Michaeltown.'

Fiunella told Gilbert that the Earl and his party were riding across a meadow where cattle were grazing and his horse trod in a cowpat and slipped. Unfortunately the horse threw its rider against an outcrop of rock and his neck was broken.

She looked up at Gilbert and asked, 'Do you ride a horse?'

'No, I prefer to drive a car,' he replied.

'Oh, so lightning can't strike twice,' Fiunella said.

'Thankfully not,' he added.

Gilbert read further, 'Fiunella FitzMichael, Countess of Dunrea, born 1151 the daughter of Conel O'Brian, Chieftain of lands in Dunrea. Died 1223.'

He had brought a camera with him and Fiunella took a photograph of him standing by the tomb.

'Tell you want. Let's have a photograph taken together in case we were these two in a former life.'

'But we're not married,' she replied.

'More's the pity,' he answered.

'Are you married?' she asked.

'Yes, but my wife does not share my enthusiasm for family history.'

Fiunella sighed, 'What a shame.'

'How about that photograph?' he asked.

'OK then,' she answered.

Gilbert called over an attendant and asked him if he would take their photograph. The man duly obliged.

Later, as they strolled back to the car, Gilbert stopped to admire a statue of St Kieran and a wolfhound.

'I suppose he was a bit like St Bernard,' he commented.

'Not really,' Fiunella replied. 'Although he did breed wolfhounds, the locals jokingly call the statue, 'The priest with the beast'.'

Driving back to Michaeltown a fateful occurrence took place. A herd of cattle blocked the road and once the way was clear again Gilbert impatiently pushed the accelerator down hard. The car skidded on a pile of cow dung and overturned by the side of the road. They both managed to scramble out and Gilbert took Fiunella in his arms, kissed her and breathed, 'Déjà Vu?'

FOUR DOWN TWO ACROSS
Ruth Locker-Smith

'A blind date! You must be joking,' looking at Sonia's determined face
I realised this wasn't one of her little jokes.

'Well what have you planned for me?' my grudging tone gave her
the cue to carry on,

'Sally, it's for your own good, you've been on your own for several
months now, it's time to move on.'

'Please don't remind me,' my mind flashing back on the day Dave,
my ex boyfriend, made his last visit to my florist shop. I should have
realised something was amiss when I laughingly said, 'You have a
guilty look about you.'

A bright pink blush spread across his face. 'I'm here to tell you
something,' he announced thrusting a bright yellow bunch of daffodils
into my hands, the phrase, 'Coals to Newcastle,' sprang to mind but still
it was a nice gesture.

'You've never brought me flowers before! Spit it out!' I urged,
thinking he would be working away again this weekend.

'I've been promoted!'

'That's brilliant,' I interrupted with relief as worrying doubts
crossed my mind emphasising all the worst scenarios possible.

'My training course consists of six weeks in Birmingham.'

'No problem,' I uttered trying to hide my disappointment, after all
six weeks would pass quickly, it wouldn't be the end of the world.

Dave proceeded in a somewhat mumbling voice about writing to
me, which in hindsight was odd after all phone calls would make more
sense, a quick kiss and he was off. Three days later the promised letter
arrived, tears welled up in my eyes as I recalled the words, 'Sorry, Sal,
it's for the best, I'm sure you'll thank me for giving you your freedom.'

I was about to enter my 'Sombre mood' thinking how could he have
done this to me, words I constantly used nowadays when Sonia's
exasperated voice broke into my reflections with, 'Are you listening,
Sal?'

'Yes of course.' Sonia was right. I had to move on with my life and
forget the past.

With a new positive approach I listened to my friend's explanation, 'You've met Rachel in my office, she has a cousin, Mark, we just happened to discuss you one tea break!'

How humiliating to think I was the subject of office gossip. Oh well I'll go along with Sonia's plan if it makes her happy, after all, I figured, I owed her big time, she is my one true friend who encouraged me to go on when I needed a shoulder to cry on and let's face it, cry I did!

Eagerly she described her plan, her enthusiasm was catching and maybe her brainwave wouldn't be so bad after all. Operation 'Blind Date' was to commence this coming Wednesday.

Entering my flat after a busy day the noise of the telephone greeted me. Picking up the receiver Sonia's excited voice sang down the line, 'Now you're not getting butterflies are you, Sal?'

'Course not,' I replied ignoring the rumble my stomach gave.

'I've met Rachel's cousin a couple of times,' she continued, 'he seems to be a decent bloke. Don't forget - seven o'clock at Samuels, must dash my cats, Scampi and Rizzo, are pleading for their food, good luck and by the way of thanks I'll be happy to be your chief bridesmaid!'

I laughed at the last remark, placing the receiver down my smile faded from my face, was it possible to remember any of Sonia's matchmaking which had blossomed into romance? No was the answer. Oh well the law of averages suggested she had to be right one day, let's hope today would be it! I ran my bath, the enjoyment of a long soak, candles flickering inviting a relaxing atmosphere. I couldn't remember the last time I had treated myself to such luxury, the warmth of the water, the tranquillity and peaceful ambience began to have the desired effect - my eyes were closing, about to drift off. My senses were brought suddenly to life like a jolt of electricity. There was no time to dream, preparation for my date was necessary. What to wear? This was every girl's nightmare especially for a first meeting. Searching through my wardrobe rejecting almost every garment, I settled for my favourite black dress, its sophisticated design always made me feel more confident.

Arriving at seven o'clock I stepped inside Samuels my eyes adjusting to the brightness within, two magnificent floral displays stood either side of the entrance arranged on huge pedestals wafting their delicate fragrance bringing a sense of delight. My skills in floral design encouraged an overpowering desire to rearrange two offending blooms misplaced in the midst of such splendour. With sudden impulse I deftly placed flowers and nearby foliage into their correct position feeling satisfaction no one had observed me. This assumption was incorrect - one handsome diner saw the spectacle, giving me an understanding smile.

I completed my final check, smoothing out an imaginary crease in my dress, inspecting my shoes satisfied the heels were high enough to ensure a total ensemble of elegance. I couldn't have been more ready apart from the lurch of apprehension in my stomach. My date would be holding The Times newspaper, his attention on the crossword. Glancing anxiously around my eyes rested on a very handsome man seated in a secluded corner of the restaurant. Surely this couldn't be my date, propped up against the centre floral display on his table lay the Times newspaper. With a dry mouth my confident resolve was disappearing fast. Feeling a large amount of trepidation I found myself heading in his direction.

'Hello there, are you Mark?' I marvelled at the steady tone of my voice considering the state my nerves were in.

'Yes, I'm Mark, hello to you too!' he replied, the richness of his voice sounded deep and sensuous.

'Um, may I sit down?'

'Please do.'

Thankfully I sat down, my legs had suddenly acquired a tremble. 'I've never done this before,' I explained, 'My friend, Sonia, persuaded me.'

'Well, my gratitude to her! Would you care to tell me about yourself?'

Embarking on my life story I hardly paused for breath. Oh dear, I had promised myself a dignified explanation instead of which I was chatting away as if I had known him all my life. 'So there you are!' concluding my tale, 'All my past history leading up to this blind date.' Realisation was dawning, Dave had never listened to me as Mark had done. This was quite a new experience. I found myself making comparisons. Dave's prediction was starting to ring true, I was glad to be free. Silently I applauded Sonia, she had definitely excelled herself this time. I would never doubt her match making skills again.

Mark broke into my reverie stating, 'Excuse me one moment, a colleague of mine needs my attention, I'll be back shortly.'

Picking up the menu I studied the tempting dishes on offer and realised how hungry I was, when out of the corner of my eye someone was making a beeline towards my table. A tall awkward looking man stopped nearby.

'You must be Sally, my blind date! I recognised you from Rachel's description.'

The full impact of my error hit me, how embarrassing I'd chatted up the wrong man! What was I to do? Thankfully that decision was taken out of my hands when Mark interrupted, 'The lady is with me.'

'Oh, sorry mate, my mistake.' Backing away he nearly collided with the waiter whereupon he made a hasty retreat.

I gave an inquiring look at Mark.

'I know what you're thinking - I'm just a swine.'

Gazing into his expressive brown eyes it was difficult to remain angry.

'I never sought to deceive you, my name is Marcus, my friends call me Marc, I always dine here but today my work commitments resulted in a late booking which I will always be grateful for because I spotted this beautiful girl who looked so vulnerable, yet maintaining a controlled excitement. I knew I couldn't let her go!'

Marc reached out, touching my hand. No other words were necessary. My heart melted as Marc pointed to the clues of the crossword he had completed which stated, 'Four down, a five letter word meaning visual beauty,' two across 'A two lettered inscription meaning a method of signing off.' With bold letters it read 'Sally XX.'

THE THIRD DRAWER DOWN
Thelma Kellgren

It had taken Nancy a long time to be at peace with herself over being a Baptist minister's daughter. How she could remember her father's severe features, his complete lack of humour and her fear when as a child she had to sit in the front pew. The church was always cold even in summer and as she listened to her father rant about sin, Hell and damnation it became even colder. The Devil was no mythical figure to her, he pursued her in the dark. Although she felt that she had now put the devil behind her she wondered whether this was ever entirely possible! Her mum was sweet and kind and tried to be comforting but now that she, herself, was thirty-five she realised that her mother, too, was a little frightened of the man. Being an only child hadn't helped as there was no one to confide in - no one to giggle with.

Her teenage rebellion, she now realised, was exaggerated by the very fact of her situation and it had taken her many years to sort herself out. As a very little girl, who had tried so hard to be 'good', she felt very resentful at being called 'sinful'. What did he want? Because of the confusion in her mind she gave very little thought to what was actually being said in church and in Bible lessons. She seemed to be eternally perplexed. Even when she was baptised in the tank, under the pulpit, she doubted what was going on and felt it to be a charade. She now really regretted the opposition and difficulties she had caused her mother when all the while it was her father she hated. Hate? Was it too strong a word? Yes, perhaps so, as after his death she was able to get her feelings in perspective. Poor man - what had been his problem?

Nancy had been determined to go to university and thoroughly enjoyed her course even though her parents had opposed her choice. At university she seemed to have room to breathe and made friends with people from a great variety of backgrounds.

Computer science with its technological and scientific content had suited her down to the ground and she had no difficulty obtaining a 2-1. Suitable employment was not difficult in this rapidly expanding field and by the time she and Bill were married she was well settled into the firm.

She and Bill had met at a very 'swish' drinks party and they had drifted toward one another quite automatically as neither was quite sure what they were doing there. It was a very up-market do, the engagement party of a friend Nancy had made at university but had never quite realised how well off she was.

She felt it wasn't really her scene and was relieved when Bill looked after her during the evening. He was there reporting the affair for the local paper. It seemed quite natural that she should agree to his seeing her home and that they should make a date for the coming weekend.

Bill was so easy; a well-educated man, a broad thinker, an agnostic who was gentle and amusing. They soon graduated from easy going companionship to love and this had grown stronger with the years. She had been surprised at how well Bill and her father got on. After her father's death they had moved her mother to a small flat nearby. It was within convenient walking distance and now that Ben was six and Tom eight it had been safe for them to visit her on their own. They had loved their gran a lot and loved visiting her and her death had upset them greatly.

After the funeral Ben said, 'Tell me about dying, Mum, why do we have to do it?'

Answering that was difficult but clearing out the flat was really awful. She and Bill had been at work on the flat for a week and they were both really tired. One night Bill walked in from work and started arguing straight away.

'Nancy, why couldn't you listen to me? We could have avoided all this if we'd had a house clearance firm in!' He flopped in a chair.

'You know I wanted to sort her things out myself - I miss her.'

'Yes, alright, alright,' his voice raised, 'but this is only making you feel worse.'

'Oh shut up and help me.'

'Help you?' he shouted. 'How the hell can I help you when you object to everything I suggest?'

She heard herself screaming back, 'If you made any sensible suggestions, you selfish b*****d, perhaps I would listen to you.'

His face whitened as he said, 'And we're not having that bloody chest of drawers.' He kicked the chest and slammed out the door.

Nancy collapsed in a heap and looked at the chest. What was happening? She seemed to have lost complete control of herself. *Oh Bill, dear Bill, I need you.*

Thank Heaven the boys had slept through the row but where the devil had Bill gone? To the pub probably. She wept at the thought of their slanging match. And now, oh dear, there was the news of this pregnancy just when everything seemed to be going so well. Although she adored her boys, she herself had secretly hoped that one of them would be a little girl. Perhaps this was her little girl. This would mean that she would have to be off work for some time but what about Bill's job? He had always longed to write and was quite good but 'quite good' is not enough in an overcrowded field. He had been a reporter on the Echo for some years, wrote a lot in his spare time and his head was full of ideas. He had recently had a script accepted by ITV and was convinced that he could become an independent scriptwriter given half a chance. How she remembered the night that they had discussed the matter endlessly, trying to explore all the ramifications. Bill had tried, very hard, not to let her see how much it mattered to him. At last it had been decided that he would resign his job and they would live on her salary. They had gone to sleep wrapped in each other's arms.

Ben, her youngest, had been at school for a year; they had taken a deep breath and a large mortgage and bought a house that they all loved. It was not grand but substantial, with three good bedrooms and a garden that gave the boys plenty of scope for play. Nancy just could not decide how she felt about this pregnancy - if only her mother was here for her to talk it over with . . . she wept again. She herself could not understand why she felt so strongly about having her mother's old chest. It was a good solid looking piece of furniture of no great value but it seemed to have a character of its own. It impressed itself upon you when you entered a room where it stood. True, it didn't fit in with their present bedroom furniture but really what a fuss. Perhaps it was having something intimate and sentimental of her mother's whom she had loved so much.

As soon as Bill came in an hour later, seemingly calm and contrite she told him about the pregnancy. She was speechless at his reaction with no thought of her at all. Could this be her devoted, reasonable husband whom she loved so much? It was as though he'd had a personality change as he started to rant and this time the boys did wake up. They stopped quarrelling to comfort the boys but it all started again as soon as they got into bed.

'It is just not on to have another child and you to be off work with all our financial commitments! I know, I just know that I can make it as a scriptwriter but not that fast. Don't you care about me at all?'

She was so crushed she could not reply and tried to change the subject to allow things to cool down; but he just started off again and 'that awful chest of drawers' entered frequently into the harangue. They turned their backs on each other and tried to sleep. Nancy wept quietly into her pillow.

There was no conversation between them the next morning as Bill went off to work and she took the boys to school. It was a beautiful morning and Nancy could not believe that her circumstances and this lovely world could be so at odds. She decided to spend the day at home to try to sort herself out in peace and quiet and rang into work pleading illness. She tried to divert her thoughts with another cup of coffee and a look at the paper but it was no use.

Perhaps she should do some housework. With the greatest difficulty she shoved the furniture in their bedroom around to make room for the chest. They would have to get their friend, Charlie, to help them get it upstairs, as upstairs it was going - come Hell or high water. She started to clear out the drawers with very mixed feelings. All the clothes were going to Oxfam but the sentimental things were the hard bit. She opened a big black bin bag on the floor beside her. She really should have a box of Kleenex at hand.

The top drawer was not too bad as it was mostly personal hygiene things and some unopened packages of Yardley's soap that her mother so loved and thought was too expensive to use. She was of the generation that still wore stockings and also had a lot of lovely handkerchiefs. Nancy would keep these hankies. There in the corner lay the very first letter that Nancy, aged five, had written to her. What was this? Somebody's diary and upon opening it she discovered that it was her gran's. How interesting - she must keep this.

The second drawer down was undies and nighties; well mended and familiar. To her immense surprise she found a bunch of letters from her father to her mother, tied with the traditional blue ribbon. Love letters? From her father? Impossible! She had the awareness to be startled by her own reaction; she was startled by a lot of things these days.

Some dried pressed flowers, her old school reports, a painting she had once done for her mother. It seemed as though her mum had kept every little scribble that Tom and Ben had ever written her. There, to her surprise, were her pig-tails cut off when she was ten and carefully kept in a silk bag.

The third drawer down seemed to be mostly woollies and blouses. Each drawer was carefully fitted with faded wallpaper that belonged to quite another age. All this stuff could go in the Oxfam bag. As she pulled out the last jumper the lining paper came up with it. Reaching to put it back Nancy saw a large envelope under the paper. Upon opening it she was speechless: it contained £100 worth of Marks and Spencers original scrip issue shares on which No divided had ever been paid. Clearly marked with her mother's name, they must be worth a fortune. How had her mum ever dared purchase these without her dad knowing?

Oh dear old chest of drawers - oh dear old Mum! She shouted and danced round the room and was tempted to ring Bill at the office but thought better of it and relished the thought of breaking the news tonight. Bill? Oh dear - the memory of their morning parting was painful. What was happening to them and how was she going to put it right? She made herself a cup of tea and sat down to meditate. The last fortnight had been a real test and trial for them and she was not exactly proud of the way she had been behaving. She realised that until Bill came into her life she had never felt like a whole person or really loved. His love for her had allowed her to release her own emotions and experience security she had never known. What was she doing jeopardising this?

As she sat she realised that no amount of money could replace this and that all that mattered was her husband and their children. Yes, of course, the money would be helpful but it was not what life was about. Some of her father's comments and sermons came into her mind and she was aware that it hadn't all been wasted on her. Absentmindedly she reached over and took the blue ribboned bunch of letters onto her lap. Withdrawing one and starting to read she was carried back to her parents' meeting. This man revealing to this woman that he had never felt loved by anyone until he met her and she and his religion had given him the strength to live. She discovered that his father had been a brutal, cold-hearted man who beat him interminably. His mother had turned a blind eye to it all and implied that it was deserved. As a very small child he had been thrown into the cellar semi-conscious and not allowed out until he said he was sorry. For what he never knew and after all his suffering he had found her. It was more than he deserved. His adolescence had been shy and troubled and girls had been just too frightening. Then she had come along and it was like being given a second chance. How could he ever express his love for her?

By this time Nancy was sobbing and all the tensions of the past fortnight welled up in her. How very complicated life is - imagine growing up with this man and never understanding him at all. He had kept it all to himself. It had been a sobering and instructive day. She so wished she could talk to him. She closed her eyes and said aloud, 'I'm so sorry, Dad.'

MY FIRST LOVE
Michael McNulty

I was fourteen when I had to go for an ear operation. The specialist sent me to the Liverpool Children's Hospital and my operation was set for Tuesday. The surgeon wanted me to come in on Monday though so they could make sure I fasted for twenty-four hours.

I had all my things packed on Sunday night and the next morning we left Frodsham in my mother's car at nine. We hit a traffic jam at the Runcorn Bridge.

We finally arrived at the hospital at half past ten. A nurse ushered us to my ward and another showed us to my bed. My mother helped me to unpack and then left me.

As I made my way to the television room I heard someone crying. I opened the door and popped my head in. There was someone in a bed lying face down crying into a pillow to cover the noise.

'Would you like me to get a nurse for you?'

When the person moved their head off the pillow and turned to face me, I could see it was a girl.

'No thank you,' she replied in between sobs.

'Is there anything I can do for you?' I asked trying to be friendly.

'Yes there is, you can get out of my room and leave me alone,' she yelled at me.

'Sorry I bothered you, goodbye.' I closed the door and went in the television room. There was nobody in there so I had a cigarette.

It was about an hour later when that girl came into the room. She had long brown hair and was about five foot seven. She was very pale and very skinny, yet if she had a few more stone on her she would be beautiful. She had on a blue pair of jeans and a white baggy jumper and she smelt of perfume.

'I am sorry about before, please forgive me, by the way, my name is Lynne Clark.' She walked over to me with her hand held out.

I shook her hand and told her, 'It should be me apologising to you, after all I invaded your space. By the way, my name is Victor Cordell and I'm pleased to meet you.'

She let go of my hand and sat down next to me. 'I've not seen you before, what are you in for?'

'I'm having an operation on my left ear. What about you?'

'I've been here off and on for over four years. I've been suffering from bulimia nervosa and anorexia.' She got up and went out the room. I went back to my bed and just stayed there until they came around with the dinner trolley. Then I went back in the television room for another cigarette. At about two I knocked on Lynne's door.

'Who is it?'

'It's me, Victor. I was wondering if you want to play a game of something, I have nothing to do.'

'Yes sure, come on in.'

I opened the door and walked over to her bed. As I got near her she patted the mattress telling me that's where she wanted me to sit.

'Well what would you like to play?' I asked as I made myself comfortable on her bed.

'Can you play Chinese patience?'

'Yes, so I take it we're playing that, and you can deal.' While she was dealing I asked her, 'What made you want to lose weight at such an early age?'

This was her reply. 'When I was ten, I was about six pounds overweight and when I went to join the dancing class, the tutor pointed that out to me. She told me that I would never become a dancer unless I lost some of those pounds. That's when my peers began to stereotype me as 'fatty'. They would call me other horrible names as well, so I stopped eating and I exercised every day. Then one day I collapsed and they brought me here.'

She started to cry on my shoulder. I put my arms around her skinny body and just left her there. When she had finished I gave her a hankie. She dried her eyes and blew her nose, then she kissed me on the lips.

'What was that for?' I asked sounding surprised.

'I don't know, I just felt like it.' I put my hand on her face and then we started necking.

We had just started playing cards when the nurse walked in. 'You out, you're not allowed in here!' she shouted. Then as I was walking out I heard her say to Lynne, 'You never ate your dinner again today so you're not allowed to leave your room or see anybody.'

I just stayed in my ward until one in the morning. I could not sleep with all the other kids crying, so I went for a smoke. On my way past Lynne's room I gave her a knock. She followed me into the television room.

'Would you like one of these?' I asked as I handed the packet over to her.

'No thanks, I do not smoke. I tried it once, my face turned green and I was sick everywhere.' Lynne came over to me and sat on my knee and started to kiss me. After I had finished my cigarette I went back to my room and Lynne went to hers.

The operation was successful and when I came around I went to see Lynne. There was a doctor going into her room, so I went into the television room and waited until he had left. Lynne ran into the television room. She saw me and ran straight over and jumped on my knee and started crying on my shoulder again.

'What's wrong Lynne? Who's upset you now?' I could not get any sense out of her so I just held her in my arms. She cried herself to sleep.

When she finally woke up there were other people in the room so we could not talk there. We could not go in her room so I took her outside where we could be alone.

'You know when I told you that I was bulimic; well I missed loads out. I used to take four hundred laxatives a day and I was taking eight proplus a day as well which kept me awake so I could do more exercises. I had taken slimming tablets as well and I have just found out that now I have got liver damage. The doctor has just told me. He said that if I do not get a liver donor I would die within a year. It's not fair, you're the only boy who has taken any interest in me and you're the only boy I have ever kissed properly, now I'm going to lose everything.'

She started crying again.

'Look, I'm sure someone will donate a liver to you, there are hundreds of people dying everyday. I'm sure someone will be able to match your blood group,' I told her trying to reassure her.

'When are you going home?'

'In five days. Why?'

'I promise you that I will eat all my meals so I can spend the last five days with you,' she said trying to cheer herself up.

That night I tried to imagine myself in a situation like that and how I would handle it. Would suicide enter the equation or would I let everybody who loved me suffer and watch me die or would I run away and tell nobody and die a lonely death? I'm glad I don't have to make that choice. Yet Lynne has to face that every day now.

The remaining five days I spent with Lynne we had a laugh, fooling around and doing stupid things, she had a great sense of humour. Half the time you would have thought we'd been drinking or taking drugs, but we did not do either. We would play jokes on the others like putting water balloons on top of the doors and watching somebody get wet. At night-time Lynne and I would have wheelchair races until we got caught then we would walk around the hospital. Having a conversation on anything and everything or we would delve into each other's private life to get to know each other a bit better.

On the night before I left, Lynne and I swapped addresses and telephone numbers. We gave each other a goodbye kiss there and then. I had to start my packing soon, so I would not have time to see her later.

When I got back to Frodsham I could not stop thinking about Lynne. It was the best week I'd had in a long time.

The next morning I was up at seven and after my shower and breakfast I went and knocked on everyone's door that had a car in their drive. I offered to wash it for one pound. One bloke gave me a five-pound note because I did an excellent job. After my dinner I went round the other half of the estate offering to cut their grass. I got the odd comment here and there.

'Why are you not in school?' they would ask.

'I've been expelled so I'm doing anything to stay out of my mother's way,' was my reply. I thought it would give them something to gossip about.

By Friday I had earned over one hundred and fifty pounds. That is with people giving me extra than what I had asked for, so the next morning I told my mother that I was going to my friend's house and I managed to get the first H21 to Liverpool, from outside the Bears Paw.

'One half to Liverpool town centre please?' I asked as I was getting my money out of my pocket.

'That will be one pound twenty please,' the bus driver said as he was doing my ticket. I got my ticket and change and went and sat down at the back of the bus.

When I got off the bus an hour and a half later, the rain was coming down heavy. I stayed in the bus shelter until it had stopped.

When I got to see Lynne, she was so weak she had to be pushed in a wheelchair by a nurse. I told her that I was falling in love with her and I just wanted to be with her.

'I thought once you went back home, when you saw your mates again, you would forget about me, so I went and took an overdose. I had to have my stomach pumped. I could not live if you weren't in my life. I know that I have only known you a week, but I have had more fun in one week than I have had in my whole life. You made me so happy, now I have got only literally hours left. Please don't let me die in this place?' The tears were running down her face.

'Well nurse, can I bring her back when it's all over?' I asked.

'All right, go on then.'

When we got outside it was not raining, so I pushed her down to the Pier Head and we took a ferry across the Mersey. Lynne managed to get out of the wheelchair and sit on my knee. We started kissing, then she pulled away. 'I love you. Now that I'm really happy, my life is over. I'm sorry that we never met a few years back, then I wouldn't be in this mess. I want you to have this.' She took off her gold cross and passed it to me.

'Thank you, I will never take it off,' I told her.

'I love you so much, goodbye.' Then she died in my arms. I cried pushing her all the way back to the hospital.

FLAMES OF DESTINY
Tony Gyimes

It was 64AD, the tenth year of the reign of the tyrant Nero. Amid soaring temperatures of early summer and the murderous activities of the emperor, the lawyer Nestos Dormontes entertained. Whispers about the conduct of Nero were spreading quickly along the streets of Rome. According to them, he had killed his mother and a number of other people, enough for the lifetime of several emperors. It was dangerous even to listen to such talk, for the chances of defending someone against charges of conspiracy were nil. As a lawyer, Nestos was well aware of that. Fortunately his elegant hillside villa stood some distance from the capital, so he and his guests felt protected from both the heat of the city and its whispers. No wonder that the friends of the lawyer enjoyed themselves in the portico consuming large amounts of food and drink. Two young servants, a boy and a girl, were in constant attendance refilling dishes and drinking vessels. The girl, Seremis, came from Egypt. The boy, renamed Galgus by the lawyer, came from a Mediterranean island. What no one knew was the love the servants had for each other. The people present, including the lawyer, did not really care. Nestos was looking forward to the summer days without any court cases. He can then frequently invite friends to his house. While there they could feel both cool and safe, whereas Rome was hot and dangerous. So with two young servants at his disposal, why should he not enjoy himself.

Although unmarried, he was far from being too old to deny himself certain pleasures of life. The nights in his house were not just pleasant, but also something special. Rarely without surprises, he wanted to provide his guests with entertainment as they ate their meal.

He gave instructions to the girl in that sense. 'Dance Seremis! Entertain, be charming and capture their attention.'

Seremis protested in vain that she was not skilled in that profession. Her pleas were dismissed.

'Everything can be learned,' her master insisted. 'In any case, I've already hired musicians with whom you'll have plenty of time to practise.'

There was no escape for her. As soon as the hired musicians arrived she had to start practising with them. Although unskilled in the art of entertainment, Seremis adapted her dance to their style of music which sounded strange to an Egyptian. In spite of her inexperience, her performances, either as a mermaid or a goddess of love, were popular with the friends of Nestos. Never before had the lawyer received so many congratulations and expressions of delight from the audience. He was also aware of the longing glances directed at Seremis as she danced. Noticing the attention focused on her, Galgus could barely contain his anger. As a slave he had no power to alter anything, but Galgus left the girl in no doubt about his dismay.

'How long will this go on?' he demanded of her.

'How can I answer that? Am I not a slave like you?' she replied.

'You seem to enjoy exposing yourself to those parasites. It is as if you and I had never met.'

Seremis called to mind those mornings of delight they had shared together.

'Don't be too angry with me. I too feel the strain of it all.'

For Galgus, riddled with jealous rage, this was not enough. 'Listen to me,' he warned her, 'if I ever see one of those fat clowns reaching for you, I'll squeeze the breath out of him. I won't care what happens to me afterwards. Do you understand?'

His physique showed that he was capable of carrying out his threat.

'Don't talk like that please?' she begged him. His eyes revealed his true feelings.

The musicians helped Seremis by playing tunes she could adapt to her dances which expressed sadness, defiance and hope for change. Although not a skilled dancer her body language captivated the audience. The well-to-do Romans had no interest in the fate of slaves and were only vaguely interested in the actual dances. There was an exception, one of her audience, his mind sharper than the rest, could see what her dances were about. Some evenings later, in July 64AD, after a very hot day, Seremis learnt his identity.

A refreshing breeze after sunset brought a movement of cool air through the portico. Seremis was surprised to see only Galgus present. He was busy lighting torches that were to be placed on the garlanded tables. He worked in silence and on completing his task left, without looking or speaking to her. Puzzled by his behaviour, Seremis did not know what to do. Dressed as she was, as an Egyptian, how could she perform when no one was present. A chill ran through her senses at the thought that she may be on her own in the villa when someone approached her from the house - it was her master Nestos. Elegantly dressed, his thin hair shiny and scented, the lawyer invited her to sit at a table.

'What table?' she asked.

'The table of your choice. Tonight you can decide what you want to do.'

This puzzled Seremis even more. 'I don't understand. I came here to dance and only we are present.'

'No one is invited so you won't be dancing tonight,' Nestos informed her.

He clapped his hands and Galgus appeared, carrying dishes containing food which he served to them. He served them in silence. Seremis noticing the brooding look in his eyes, felt that something ominous was looming, looming like the shadows of the columns of the portico as they fell across the place. She thought it strange that Nestos wanted to spent time with his slave, the truth began to dawn on her a little later. Before retiring, he sent her to fetch some wine. She filled a neat, bronze vessel with wine and took it to his heavily-scented room. He lay fully clothed on his bed. As she placed the wine close to him he appeared to be gazing at the torchlight, in truth his eyes were absorbing her presence. In the flickering flame her figure seemed blurred especially her face. The Egyptian costume she wore created an air of mystery, evoking a spirit too ancient to exist. Pouring wine into his cup he said casually, 'It is not often that a servant is given the privilege of spending the night with her master. Yet, that is what I'm offering you now. What is your response?'

They both knew that he had carefully chosen this way instead of ordering her to fulfil a duty. Yet it took her by surprise. Not so much the proposal, but rather the timing. The lawyer was irritated by the lack of enthusiasm displayed by the slave to his offer.

'Now I want you to think carefully,' he said. 'Your position does not allow you to refuse my offer.'

Seremis answered defiantly. 'I know where I am and what I am. I know that you have sole authority over my life, but there is one thing even you can't take away from me.'

The torchlight revealed the determination in her face. 'That one thing is who I decide to spend the night with. Apart from my duties, I'd never want to be alone in this room with you.'

Nestos jumped up and hissed. 'Duties! It is the duty of a slave to please her master when so ordered.'

Seremis remained adamant. 'You can do what you like . . . you can threaten to kill me, but I won't change what I have said.'

Nestos, agitated, raised his voice. 'Do you know I can send you back to the slave market, or I might be able to make you a free person?'

Either proposition would mean she would lose Galgus. *I would rather die than be separated from Galgus,* she thought.

Enraged by her silence Nestos reached for her and began to rip at her veils, demanding obedience. Seremis suddenly took up the bronze wine vessel and struck her tormentor on the head. He crashed to the floor, blood gushing from a deep wound to his head mingling with the wine.

In a highly emotional state, she screamed, 'Me and Galgus are in love!'

Her words fell on dead ears.

She began to think of the consequences of her actions. Someone else in her position might have given into his demands, but this is what she has done. There was no turning back. The commotion brought Galgus to the bedroom. 'Come . . . let us get out of here.'

As they stepped out onto the torchlit portico, Seremis had to sit down. Leaning against a column she felt weak and began shivering. 'I know what I've done. A slave has killed her master. There's only one thing I can do now.' She thought for a moment then smiled, 'A well-mixed draught will do it quickly . . . and I know how to mix it.' She looked at Galgus. 'The best thing for you to do would be to run away! To make yourself free!' she paused for breath. 'If they find you here with two bodies they'll accuse you of murder. A slave can expect no mercy. You'd be put to death, probably after terrible torture.'

Galgus shook his head, loud voices from outside cut short his answer. He became aware of people from the nearby villas running towards a viewpoint on the hillside, shouting as they did so, 'Fire! Fire! The circus is burning.'

'Fire! What fire?' The slave asked himself. He told Seremis to remain where she was until he returned. A number of people were present at the spot which provided a good view of Rome. What they witnessed took their breath away. One end of the Circus Maximus was on fire and it appeared to be spreading rapidly, first to the opposite hill then to the nearest, winding streets. Many of the houses were constructed of light mortar which caught the flames within minutes. Soon large numbers of city dwellers became trapped by walls of flames which cut off their escape routes. The once quiet night echoed to the terrified death cries of Romans as they became human torches. The fire quickly spread to other parts of the city causing carnage and even more victims. Many people on the hillside feared that the flames would catch up with them too. Galgus had seen enough. Back at the house he told Seremis about the unfolding catastrophe that threatened Rome with destruction. 'It seems unstoppable.'

The girl urged him to leave. 'This is your chance to flee. For the sake of our love and the happiness we have shared, please go! Go now! While there is panic, no one would notice you . . . let me see you leave this place.'

Galgus shook his head. 'I cannot quite get what you're talking about. Do you really want me to vanish?'

'Yes! Yes! Please hurry,' she urged.

'Well, I'd only do that if you came with me as well.'

The girl protested. 'But I would be a burden on you.'

Galgus nodded. 'If so we'd share that burden.'

Seremis still had doubts. 'Where could we go then?'

'Any escape is risky. We must try to get out of Rome first then make our way to my island homeland. From there you might have a chance to return to your own country.'

The girl did not answer. Even the vague hope of seeing her homeland again was enough to change her mind so she nodded her agreement.

Galgus found gowns and hoods for them both, and they hurriedly left the house. The young couple made their way to the opposite slope of the hill in the direction of the Ostia Gate. As they did so, amid terrified death cries, the City of Rome was gradually turning into a cemetery of flames.

THE BOY ON THE BRIDGE
F A C

Katherine Holmes was daydreaming as to whether 'the boy on the bridge' still existed. The bridge had been near her parent's house in the Eastern Highlands of Zimbabwe. The boy was her first connection with a young male adult. Their home had been built in the bungalow chalet style, with two wings attached by a covered way, as was the custom to safeguard against hordes of ravenous termites.

On the outset of the Holme's first visit to Inyanga, where their introduction to that magnificent range of mountains had been made welcoming and comfortable in a well established family run guest house, it had been mooted that it would be a good idea to have another similar establishment to take an overflow of guests. The word would then spread on bush telegraph for African miles of the great hospitality to be had in those panoramic mountains 6,000 feet above sea level. There was no bilharzia in the icy, fast flowing rivers, no dangerous mosquitoes and a marvellous climate.

The sun blazed out of a peerless blue sky, the house servants were friendly and much loved. At times the nights were frosty enough to warrant the lighting of a wattle log fire.

The rain appeared on cue, heralding them would be swarm upon swarm of flying ants. The dry, brown bush turned luminous it seemed in a matter of hours producing extravagant clumps of wild canary yellow Arum lilies, bright red and yellow red-hot pokers, and other transitional plants that were poised to bloom at this moisture-laden time, plus of course, brilliant green kikuyu grass.

Katherine rode native ponies with her friends on Western style saddles, acting out familiar childhood versions of 'Cowboys' and 'Indians'. Their freedom kissed God's lips, they were benign and hallowed. Boarding school and a latent Victorian rigidity marred these exotic times. 'You will conform'.

In the little chapel on Sundays devout concentration was encouraged all the more not just by the vicar, or imagined bible scenes, but from the breathtaking view framed in plate glass window set behind the altar. It was a focus onto far off plateaus and the formidable range of mountains of Portuguese East Africa - a permanent living reminder of the Creative Hand.

During one summer holiday 'the boy on the bridge' came to stay with his family. He was tall and already well-built, with an open friendly face, and Katherine thought, so mature. She even recalled him lighting up a cigarette after dinner along with almost all the other adults.

'Off to bed with you now darling,' said her mother. 'See you in the morning!'

During a communal walk the next day a memorable event occurred.

This particular walk included a wooden bridge which although not particular high, was nevertheless strung over fast flowing water and many of the slats were loose or missing. David, the boy, was aware of Katherine's total terror, and her attempts to be brave for her thirteen years; he knew her panic within. How could she have appealed to this kindly, gentle young man? She was so gauche and under-developed, so at a loss with this stranger who had time for her. Nothing about her said 'woman'. It all cried out 'stupid', 'wet', 'scared child' - spoiling everyone else's fun.

He picked her up and carried her across; he did not have to be asked or be reminded on the return either; the loving gesture came naturally to him. She was charmed by this, and countless years later she still thought of that shared innocence.

Once back at school, well into the new term, Katherine received an unfamiliar letter. It had a thick blue envelope with big, scrawly writing addressed to her. She opened it, discovering that it was from the boy, David.

'Dear Katherine, I so much enjoyed my stay at your lovely house, more especially I found myself attracted to you'.

She gasped, feeling strange.

'I wanted to carry on holding you long after we left the bridge, and I wished to stroke your lovely hair'.

Katherine blushed and carried on feeling strange; nevertheless bemused by her first letter from a boy.

'Do write back, and perhaps we could meet up at half-term, I am going to persuade my folks to stay with your family again! Write soon, do not be afraid. With love, David'.

'Dear David, yours is the first letter I have ever had from a boy. The nuns will not read this as a day girl is posting it for me. Thank you for your warm thoughts. I have been reliving that time over the bridge too. For once I was thankful that I was scared to cross - because it meant I could be close to you for a little while. I look forward very much to meeting up again over half-term. With love, Katherine'.

She still felt awkward and so unwomanly compared to some of her classmates.

However, back in the dormitory she turned to the girl in the bed next to her and asked, 'Have you ever been kissed by a boy?'

'Once at a party, by mistake, I think,' giggled the girl. 'Why?'

'There's this boy, David, I met him in the holidays, he's very grown up, about sixteen I think. Anyway, he's written to me and wants to see me again.'

Even as she spoke about David she felt excited and abashed and warm. No one saw these emotions. They were bound to be 'bad' or 'wrong'. Anything 'bad' or 'wrong' had to be worth investigation.

That Sunday she rang home and confirmed that David and family were booked for half-term. However, nothing is ever straightforward, the Reverend Mother had uttered these damning words: 'Any girl who has not completed her tennis dress in sewing class, by half-term may find herself grounded.'

Katherine's dress was still in bits. The girls were to file past the faculty in the very public place of the front hall, class by class. So, with pins and darts holding the cheap, transparent fabric together, her turn to be scrutinised came.

The little duiker buck deer that some unwitting parent had given to the school, as an abandoned kid - chose this moment to show his masculinity. Needle sharp horns at knee level, he appeared from nowhere and charged Reverend Mother's spaniel lying at her feet. Chaos reigned and the girls were shushed and shooed away. The duiker was not heard from again.

For her favourite yo-yo and two precious bars of chocolate, Katherine managed to get a girlfriend to help with finishing the dreadful dress. The nuns had bought the material in bulk. There had been nothing to commend it at all, it was slippery, transparent, frayed if you so much as looked at it, showed every sweaty hand print and creased dreadfully; if wavy hems had been al la mode, then they would have been the height of fashion. Even the girls who knew how to sew complained about the dresses. The ghastliness of them were the main topic up until that half-term.

The time to go home at last arrived. On the journey, Katherine dozed off and had a small dream. The family were in the car, but a comment was made that a bouquet of flowers had arrived for her -

'All the way from Inyanga Falls Hotel, their newly set-up conservatory, three beautiful orchids, and a wonderful box of Swiss chocolates for me.'

Katherine's mother turned around and beamed at her daughter. The girl's thoughts and emotions came flooding to the surface.

'For me? You? What - who are they from?'

'David and his family, darling.'

She recounted the dream to her parents, when they were home and unpacking the car. It was received in disinterested silence, but she did not care, as in a few hours the guests would be arriving. Imagine her surprise therefore when, come dinner time, there was still no sign of the expected family.

At about 9pm the phone rang two short rings and three long, the Holme's combination, on the party line that still existed then.

'Hello, is that the Holmes family?' asked a stranger's voice.

'Yes.'

'I have a message for you. My name is Sister Lawrence, calling from Bulawayo Hospital. The Caliphs apologise for their non-arrival. Mr Caliph has suffered a stroke.'

'Our most profound sympathy;' uttered Katherine's shocked father, 'please convey our concern.'

The next day David telephone.

'May I speak to Katherine please?'

The phone was handed to the dole-faced girl.

'How is your father David?' she asked, shaking uncontrollably.

'He died last night,' the young man's voice trembled. 'Naturally there is an awful lot to see to - hope to keep in touch.'

Katherine returned to school, shaken and deeply sad.

The housewife and daydream transformed the years back to her late teens, this time she and David were entirely alone, and he was carrying her, as before, across the bridge -

'Darling, I'm home, anything exciting happen today?' Her husband's arms circled around her and she felt his familiar closeness and the tenderness of his kiss on her neck. 'You look radiant,' he had spun her round.

'Well, you sort of came in at a precise moment in my daydream,' she looked quizzically at him, at her man's smile, and felt wonderfully warm suddenly towards men in general.

Her husband left the room to change, giving Katherine time to weave another section of the fantasy around herself:

David spoke: 'This time Katherine, we are going to stop in the middle of the bridge. I shall put you down, hold onto you, but let you realise there is little danger.'

'Only because you are near,' she whispered, and then he put her down.

'Hold gently onto the side, do not grip tightly, yes you may, if you want to, hold onto me first, then let go, experience a double sensation of my protection and your own trust not only in me, but in yourself!'

What wise words to come from someone who is not yet a man, they show an awareness far beyond his years, she thought, as not entirely at ease, the two of them rested in the middle of the wooden bridge. Shortly, he picked her up again and held her head gently against his shoulder, his lips brushed her cheek. When they arrived the other side, still carrying her, the two of them gazed into one another's eyes. Her long hair had slipped out of its ribbon, so he was in fact able now to stroke it as he had expressed a wish to do in his letter to her, written, it seemed, a hundred years before! A lock of his dark hair had fallen onto his forehead as he looked down at her. With one hand she reached up and pushed it back, he caught her hand and nibbled her fingertips. Then he kissed her eyes, her nose and her lips. The sensations were bewitching for her, eagerly her mouth stayed for a little on his, after their kiss.

Then all too suddenly, they both became embarrassed. David put her down and they carried on walking for a while in silence, gradually their hands found each other and he squeezed hers then linked his fingers through. Eventually they came to a shady spot and decided to sit. She lay back and watched the sky in speckled patterns through the lace of branches, David did the same.

'Happy?' he asked.

'Yes, very - I wish this could go on forever, no school, no parents.'

In an abstract way she looked at her watch from half past ten, it now read half past twelve.

'We'll have to be going back for lunch, David.'

The reverie departed and they stood, kissed briefly and returned, the bridge ritual taking place, once more displaying the total gentleness of the boy, 'her first boy', on the bridge. Her arms around his neck, she never wanted to let go. At least now, it was clear how in her favourite book at that far away time, 'Immortal Queen', by Elizabeth Byrd, just how Queen Mary felt when the Earl of Bothwell took over her lonely desires.

The whole secret, she surmised, of the beauty between a man and a woman, is managing to keep hold of that sacred innocence, to try to put the other's feelings first. Katherine's neighbour knocked on the kitchen window and pulled a face at her:

'Anyone in?' she asked.

ROMANCE IS A COUNTRY
Kirk Antony Watson

Prudence hit the stop button of the remote control, so that she could rest her mind from watching more of the news. She was at the brink of a daydream. Only the sound of the newsreader caused her to come back. The lasting image was perhaps the last, a raging football crowd against a sending off.

Beautiful Prudence, often chosen for her wistful beauty by quality fashion magazines as model of the year, had another agenda to deal with. She got into bed knowing that her day would be difficult.

In the morning, Prudence kept an eye out for the post. During the wait she had started to create new pictures of herself. In the mirror, she had defeated all of her fears. And it was evident in the shine in her eyes. She knew that she was a survivor and all others were dead. And none of them had an inkling about her.

Jacob, her artistic and beautiful lover, would be moving out of her life by now. They had not made up from a real split; not even after two desolate days. Prudence had started to believe that he was another person, and she had finally defeated Jacob. Yet, he used to mean the world to her. It might take all her strength to go forwards. He captivated her in his talk, his body too.

Prudence got to her post, after it had been put through the letter box but there was nothing from Jacob amongst the mailshots. As she walked into the kitchen to take some vitamins, she knew he would have got her letter. And for this, she was going to pay dearly.

Jacob was not happy to open Prudence's letter. He got to the end of her page and a half, at a thrilling speed. He thought of tearing it up too. And he had to take eight St John's Wort pills. She really knew how to menace him. In the movies she would be unclear, even though he had picked up the telephone. She would beat herself up by the end of their conversation. And, he would learn from her suicide what he had given her - love.

Prudence was close to going out, when Jacob called on the telephone. But, he did not feel her trying to stab him for this.

She was apprehensive. 'Jacob, I'm going out to power my gas meter and I want to buy Vogue because I've got some old pictures to hide from the other girls.'

'I've got Vogue,' he said.

Then he heard her silently shout out loud, 'What's the point in you using that - why don't you tell me what I've done?'

Prudence said goodbye by thanking him for reading her letter. And he knew that she meant it because she did.

Prudence felt exhilarated to be out in the street and she held onto the belief that the day would grow into an ally. She walked without the menace of Jacob's words inside her mind.

'All we do is make up demons just when everything is going great.'

At the corner she crossed the main road. Then, she rushed along Hopscotch Avenue where she felt happy, all of a sudden. It was as if a voice had spoken to her, solving all her doubts. Soon she felt relaxed. A clear head would defeat any foolish ideas she kept about trading material items for some peace of mind.

Jacob had started to cope with Prudence's letter, which he embraced more than once at the end of the day. And, it had begun a new sense of despair within him. He needed the coffee he drank in the kitchen. It made him remember: 'honey is a great painting in my opinion'. Prudence's words turned him into an argumentative being. He was unimpressed by the way alcohol worked in her system. Two days before, she had become a critic; in all but name only, so that he could not stand to be with her. She had no formal education in modern art. She had lived all her life without observing the art industry. She finished herself off by borrowing the shameful deficit. She looked like a small ogre. It was then, that he asked her whether she had a girlfriend.

At the shops, Prudence bought Vogue and Hair Flair after browsing through the best of the rest. She bought her gas units at the same time. Then, she tried to get out of the shop assistant's sight. He knew something and she could not deny it.

Romance is a country to her. A new world which deserted her. Sex is an ill wind to her. Most of all, heartbreak is a condition which stops her humanity. Prudence has run out of her spirituality. She feels as though Jacob is the cause, for he offered her little time as a lover. Prudence is caught out by his power.

Near the corner of Hopscotch Avenue, school children were coming out of two mini-buses. *They must have little hatred in their young lives,* she thought. They were organised by one male teacher. They looked up to him, and he became special before them. Prudence got passed them gently.

By now, Jacob had written down the main points from Prudence's letter. Of three, the first; she wanted to apologise. Then the next, she was still in love with him. And the last, she did not understand women. He was out of his depth at the very thought of taking her back.

Jacob found to his chagrin that Prudence was not at home when he phoned. It made him crumble inside since, by accident, he had altered his opinions of her. Now, he had to find a diversion from this sadness. And he discovered another memory as he sat beside the mobile phone.

Prudence had disliked Greta on first sight. For she had Jacob's relationship to protect from the famous beauty model. Some of the thoughts she shared with Jacob about Greta were misconstrued by him. He could cope with Greta's innocent sensuality - it was easy. However, she had a rich, powerful singing voice. And it defeated all notions that she was reasonable to look at.

If Prudence was measured by Greta's singing work, then she would always be found wanting. And, whilst she had a chance to be with her, she had begun avoiding Jacob in unseen ways. She tried to look young in front of him. Fortunately he faced it with good humour. But, when she lied to him about money she could not pay him back, he decided to lose her.

Jacob had lost his temper with them: however, there was no them. God, how she wished that he knew it. She did not earn any love by wanting to understand Greta. She dared to forget both of them just once. And it brought her self-respect into doubt.

Jacob saw her now in another perspective. In which, Greta shone and Prudence was condemned, two days away from each other had been filled by Greta's companionship. They went to a designer sale together, and they had learnt a lot about each other thanks to Prudence's absence. Jacob did not expect Greta to ignore his words to Prudence, even after he told her.

Greta had let all sentiments towards Prudence die. In fact, she was better than that because she asked Jacob not to think that she had lessened because she wanted him. And though, he was worn out by

Prudence's strict sexual politics, he did not care. Greta was fantastic company. Jacob thought that Prudence was a thief.

Prudence took the gas meter on first before she could indulge herself with a cup of tea. She was in the middle of Vogue before she understood that her mind had started to listen to the radio. The singer used words in a cruel fashion, eventually the love song made her feel stifled. 'Baby we need some time alone, so we can just breathe'.

TWO NEWCOMERS
Dennis Marshall

He was very much caught by surprise. He instinctively ducked his head as he began to wipe a sudden arc of spattered snow from his face and shoulders. Drying his face with the back of his hands he realised that a downhill skier had come to a stop not far from him. Chris Waxham had arrived the evening before in the pretty Austrian village of St Johann which nestled high in the Tyrol. Drifting snow had been cleared from the mountain road and traffic to Italy was moving again, so he had reached the Sporthotel for his winter break holiday.

The tall figure producing his snow pasting was goggled and correctly equipped, soon to be joined by a second skier.

They chatted a moment and then walked across to Chris who had been rubbing a snow dampened chamois leather over his car windows in the hotel car park, quite close to the rising end of the slope. The morning sunlight was bejewelling the snow's surface when the two skiers had taken the cable car, which lifted them giddily high over evergreen trees to the slope's start near the top of the Engadine Valley.

One of the approaching newcomers, realising what she had done by cascading Chris and his car, came over to him. She apologised in German for what she had done.

'That's quite all right, I shouldn't have been in the way,' he smiled, answering her in English scarcely realising he had done so. Helene Voss and her continental friend, Simone Duval, looked at him in genuine surprise, for neither of them had expected an Englishman to have been the victim of Helene's rather mischievous fun. In fact, German was a foreign language for both of them, since Helene was Norwegian and Simone, a French speaking Swiss young woman, although both of them quite confidently understood Chris's reply. Helene carefully removed her goggles and unveiled her attractive face and teasing eyes, so as to have a brief moment to take stock of this foreigner. A moment of unexpected though lightly handled embarrassment was soon forgotten as he introduced himself then invited them into the hotel coffee bar to show them they were forgiven. Afterwards he intended to try his borrowed skis but not on the slope the two women had used. He had to reacclimatise himself and warm up his 'out of practice' body before even attempting anything like the performance the women had exhibited.

Over coffee, Chris managed to piece together a few details about his two newly gained acquaintances. Simone had completed a language teaching course in England four years ago for her teaching in Switzerland. Amazingly, she had been to the very same Redbrick University where he had been a student some years before that. On hearing this he almost imagined he'd been reading a novel, as this seemed just like a fictional coincidence. This dark, intelligent, athletic young woman had actually been to a place he knew! That was indeed a conversation starter. She was wide-eyed with astonishment. Chris was now a journalist, so he explained how he'd actually been able to put linguistics to some practical use. They chatted good humouredly about this shrinking new world, and really amused themselves trying out four different languages. Meanwhile, Helene was taking stock of him with some interest. She was in Austria on an assignment to study continental sport hotels. She wished to find points of similarity and difference with those in her native land. He made her laugh with real interest when he told her he had once tried to play some English folk tunes on the eight stringed Hardanger fiddle in Ulvik. She was gathering up notes for her dossier on facilities, food, rooms, furniture and the night-life to take back to the land of the midnight sun.

Chris chanced to meet them both in the coffee bar again during his holiday. Helene beckoned Chris to their table with a magnificent view of mountains, woods and valleys. It was a morning they were having a break from skiing. They persuaded him into accepting a mystery tour. It would mean a car ride for them and a mountain walk for all three of them. His tour turned out to be fascinating. It terminated on a mountain side at a stone marked at the top with a circle divided in three segments. He could put one hand into three countries. Leaving his thumb in Austria, his index finger he placed in Switzerland and his second finger in Italy! It was one of those indelible moments of this holiday.

A day later he met them for evening drinks in the hotel. The very next evening they were both delighted to join him for dinner.

'Why are you alone here?' Helene asked him, sipping her aperitif.

'Oh, just the bliss of solitude,' Chris replied, not really giving much away.

'Sorry, I don't really understand your answer,' she said puzzled.

'I didn't mean to baffle you,' Chris added, 'but it is difficult to say why. Perhaps the truth is, that I am trying to forget something,' he replied.

'Or, perhaps, someone?' she quizzed gently, with her crisply regained comprehension.

'Have you been unhappy in love?' Simone asked directly.

'Can you tell?' he answered, good humouredly, with another question.

'Mais oui!' she said shrewdly. 'You made friends with us quickly, which seems to tell me that perhaps you are lonely? And your face is a little - how do you say? Sorrowful?'

'Sad, I think we would say. Um, perhaps,' he surmised.

'Ah, yes, sad,' she said. 'You look at us, yet your looks seems to go a long way over us, likely a lonely man, maybe a sailor!'

'Yes, we've been thinking of you as a sailor,' put in Helene, 'because Britain is an island, and to us you are looking to see if there are any more ships to be seen!' she added rather cleverly yet with a warm smile.

'Guess I am a lonely sailor,' he agreed, and her smile called forth a lighting in his own deep, intelligent, responsive eyes, rather amazed at her diagnosis.

'So you have come here - all on your own - don't you say? To forget her?' Simone summed up.

'Er, well,' he paused as if wrestling with awkwardness.

'Chris, if it is painful you need not say all to us, but sometimes if you speak it to strangers, you begin to feel better.'

'You sound to me, Simone, as if you, too, have something or someone to forget?'

'Oh, yes,' Simone replied openly without hesitation. 'I was living with a man in Paris during two years, but we fight, make peace, and fight again, but at last our togetherness did not last, I sink for many, many reasons. So now, I am free to come and live and do the work I like. You see, I have to travel also. Yet, sometimes to do things alone is very deeficult. Maybe you know that also?'

'Yes, it is not easy,' he agreed with her.

'And,' Simone went on, 'do you look now for someone else?' she added sweetly. 'Do you expect to find her here, at zis hotel?'

Chris was quite startled by the forthright questions of continental women.

'You're beginning to make me wonder, with your questions,' Chris said slowly but amiably. 'Perhaps I am, but I've not convinced myself that I am,' he laughed lightly.

'You see! When the smile of laughter comes back to your face, and your sorrowness, er, I mean sadness, is disappearing!' she added openly in that delightful way the French have of using English, lighting her thoughts with a winsome smile.

At their dinner rendezvous, it became clear to Chris that he had two very perceptive and intelligent women for his guests. He adjusted their chairs saying that he was delighted to have two beautiful, very talented and splendid friends as guests. He admired their dresses and adopted a very sudden directness, akin to their own, when having a conversation.

'It is always nice to have good luck!' said Helene, rather mischievously as they had entered the beautiful dining room to be the guests sharing his table. It was whilst choosing their courses from the gilded leather bound menus that Simone told him she was a vegetarian. Helene nodded, as if to say to him that he must hear why. Simone volunteered her reason.

She was a senior school girl in a party staying near an alpine lake. It was a hot afternoon. Their coach stopped in a narrow road outside a village.

Chris looked at her keenly, his mind snapping her at school in her teens, seeing her sun-bronzed and vivacious, one of a lively party in the fruit scented heat of an Italian countryside. Her youth enhanced by the sparkling flashing of her dark eyes. Her mind as sharp as an alpine peak and her personality as dynamic as sudden vistas. Simone, carefree among a bevy of youthful explorers. Quite suddenly through the coach's open windows came the odour of hot, young cattle and the raucous cries of drivers belabouring the drooling and saliva dripping calves with sticks. One animal got wedged between a post and a partly broken gateway. It was struck with a resounding wallop across the buttocks, but it could not move. The driver swore and hit it twice more viciously. It mooed in pain and fright but could not move. Finally, in exasperation, he went round and struck its head and neck to force it backwards, then thwacking its legs. This animal was one from a herd going to an abattoir nearby. The smell of sweating young cattle clung about the coach. Simone had put her head out and begged the driver to stop. He abused her vocally and grinned with a leer. Tears rose in her eyes and she sank back into her seat fuming at the sheer cruelty. Later her shock turned into a mental fixation determining her vow to become a vegetarian. All movement and singing in the coach abruptly ceased, leaving an icy, hostile silence. Many of them stunned by the frightening spectacle they had just witnessed. Simone was so angry that from then onwards she was determined to eat no more meat.

Chris was very touched by her narrative and moved by her respect for animals. It was Helene who asked him for his view.

To gain time to quickly cogitate upon an issue that he had not seriously thought about before, Chris admitted, at first, life was a complex business. He explained to her that he wished he'd met her at the end of her journey to assure her that such events were not common practice, and that now cattle and fowls are treated fairly and humanely for human consumption. He went on then to state what he believed. He thought that human beings are omnivorous. Was there not a parable about a father killing the fat calf to celebrate the return of his erring son? Then there was the miracle of feeding the five thousand and the disciples enjoying a second successful catch of fish. Chris sympathised with her profusely but he could not embrace her viewpoint. In fact, they were both intrigued by what he went on to say as the delicious food came to them. Does a woman become a plant eater solely on account of her deep seated sensitivity, because it is her body which nurtures new life? Her part in procreation is to nourish and recreate. She renews life. Isn't this why a woman especially has such a profound reverence for it? Chris told them that the few vegetarians he knew were female.

Helene shook her head rather dubiously saying it was something any person felt individually, and not necessarily to do with the female psyche.

When their delicious sweet arrived, Chris promised Simone vegetable pies, the freshest garden salads his homeland could produce, if ever she came back to England in the future. After all this she relaxed and their conversation turned to lighter things.

He danced with each of them to a lively accordion band. They watched the local log cutting competition. The lights on the bright axe-heads glinted and flashed. The scented wood chippings flew to the beat as teams in traditional dress competed against each other in time with the music. They toasted the winners.

Their evening concluded with his promise to take them to the airport at the end of their holiday. On their way there, they looked across to the Olympic downhill ski jump, admiring its dizzy height. He waved a final kiss of farewell as they entered the departure lounge. For Chris it had been an unusual and unexpected part of his holiday. Now in his pocket book he had two new names and addresses. He bit his lips in deep thought returning in his car. Would his next foreign trip be to Oslo or to Zurich?

SUMMER LOVERS
Christopher W Wolfe

Love ignored her, but Angelica was not to be denied, she knew what she wanted. Most of the night she'd gazed into his eyes, waiting, hoping, wanting. All her friends had deserted from the seaside dance hall. She was alone, or was she? Impulses told her differently, as constant suspicions aroused inside, nothing was about to get in the way of courage. Heightened by the music caressing the open space, she crossed the floor between. Bathed in love's ambience, she glided easily to his lips and smothered him. There was no going back. She begged only for the echo of his heart. With a radiance of the ever-glowing embers deep in her bosom, if only wilting beneath the sun's passion, her trembling voice patterned to the loosening of his lips. She didn't have to ask, she knew what she wanted.

'Is that how you always greet strangers?' he said, 'Jason, Jason Swift.'

There was a short pause, as though she was hypnotised.

'And you are?' Jason prompted.

'Oh sorry, Angelica Marsh, most friends call me Angel,' she said.

For a brief moment Angel suddenly realised what she'd done, and feeling more than embarrassed, tried to make her apologies and leave.

'Don't go,' said Jason, 'I want you to stay, it's not often I'm kissed by an angel.'

Angel was easily smitten. 'That's the sweetest thing anyone has ever said to me,' she said.

Jason relished the opportunity and said, 'Well, you caught me off guard, I'm usually stuck for words. Normally I'd be blushing now, or running for the nearest exit.'

That amused her, because until then, Angel thought she was the nervous one.

'So, what are you doing in a place like this?' asked Angel.

They both burst into laughter. It broke the tension.

'I thought that was my line,' replied Jason. He continued.

'Well, erm.'

Now he was stuck for words, but finally he said, 'Just waiting, hoping.' He paused, and then said, 'Wanting.'

Angel couldn't believe the words mirrored her own thoughts. This was totally unexpected. Her destiny was right here and she knew it.

'What do you do?' they both asked in perfect harmony.

They laughed again.

'I work at the local supermarket, on the checkout tills,' Angel said in first response. 'And you?' she asked again.

Jason tried desperately to think of something to impress, like a scuba diving instructor, or dolphin trainer at the marine centre. Instead he blurted out the truth.

'I'm a postman, in Levendon village, just up the road.'

Angel had remarked in her own mind, how fit and well Jason looked, when she first set eyes on him.

Jason carried on. 'I'm down here for the day, chilling out.'

He was getting more confident as their conversation continued. Inseparable, they amused themselves in sweet harmonies for an hour at least, Angel with a quiet tequila and Jason with his usual pint of lager. Occasionally, they'd get up to dance when the music spoke to them. Angel was at ease in Jason's arms, despite the fact he'd hardly danced with a woman before. Jason could only remember the time he danced with his sister-in-law at his brother's wedding, four years ago. This was different though, more intimate and he was enjoying himself. Fleeced by Angel's golden locks, he stroked gently as if mesmerised, counting each strand. Effortlessly, he wandered into Angel's eyes gathering thoughts.

In the tired hours, they left the hall, Jason with a comforting arm around Angel's shoulder, and Angel with her wings enveloped tightly round his waist.

Long the night seemed beneath the stars, as they walked, pausing in each other's arms. Filtered by the moonlit sky, they fell into Heaven and Heaven looked back.

Without warning Jason recited some words, 'Delight thy heart in Heaven's eye, oh stars and moonlit night, may love appraise the darkened sky, with everlasting light.'

Angel was taken aback, 'What?' she asked. She didn't know what else to say.

'Oh, er, nothing,' said Jason, suddenly lost for words again.

'No, go on, say it again,' said Angel.

Reluctantly, he did, although it never quite sounded the same.

'That was beautiful,' said Angel and planted a kiss tenderly on Jason's lips.

'Who wrote it?' she asked.

'Well, um, I did,' said Jason, feeling slightly nervous to Angel's response. No one had ever said anything like that about his poems before. In fact he'd only ever tried them out on his mum, and most of the time she never understood them anyway, or at best, sort of understood them.

They rested awhile on a bench, overlooking the sea, relaxed in conversation. Angel had forgotten all about her friends. She didn't care anymore, she was in the arms of the man she loved. The mid-summer night air enhanced the delicate voice, rebounding between two lovers.

It was getting on for two o'clock in the morning, the streets were practically deserted. Apart from the odd cat, rummaging through the over-spilling litter bins and leftover fish and chip papers, strewn across the road, this was a ghost town. In the background, the gentle sea surf, welcomed back and forth, on the rolling sands.

As it was the early hours of a Sunday morning, Jason was in no rush to get back home. It was his one full day off. Angel on the other hand, had to be back on the tills at 8am sharp. They had just started opening up on Sundays at the store, and she hated it. For the moment though, this was the furthest from her mind.

Jason tried his luck with another poem.

'Your eyes are like the sapphire blues,
your hair on waxen wings,
your voice as pure the dove so white,
who sings and sings and sings.'

'You're so romantic,' replied Angel with a smile, 'Is there no end to you talent?'

'Oh it's nothing really,' said Jason.

'How did you come to write poetry in the first place?' enquired Angel.

'That's a long story,' said Jason. 'I'd rather not go into too much detail, except to say. I was in love with a girl once, and basically, she wasn't interested. There were so many thoughts and ideas racing around inside my head at the time, it just seemed a natural thing to do. So a lot of my feelings ended up on paper, and it progressed from there really. I quite enjoy writing now.'

'Do you still have feelings for this girl?' asked Angel hesitantly.

'Oh no, no, God no, not anymore,' Jason replied assertively, 'That's all in the past.'

Angel was reassured, although she could see deep in Jason's eyes and sensed a hidden sadness. She questioned him no further, but took his right hand and placed it gently to her left breast, without taking her eyes off him. Jason was clearly embarrassed by this and tried to remove his hand, but Angel gripped him firmly and said simply, 'I love you Jason.'

This was all too much to take in, as tears started welling in Jason's eyes, before rolling down his cheeks.

'So do I,' he said finally.

Embroiled in time's wasted breath, Angel hesitated no longer. She kissed Jason French style, mouth to mouth, tongue on tongue. Coming up for air now and then, before resuming the depths of love. Consumed in love's desire, their hands molested and groped one another. With his light fingers, Jason squeezed and played with Angel's breasts, as her head lulled back in sheer ecstasy. Angel had never experienced anything like this before and was loving every minute.

'I want you, I need you Jason, inside me,' urged Angel between breaths.

Aided by the moonlit night, they both stumbled onto the golden sands. It was far too tempting. Languishing by the water's edge they fell into a heap. The sand was everywhere, in their shoes, their clothes, their hair. Angel tossed off her shoes whilst Jason undid his laces. Angel couldn't wait and tried to unzip her blue chiffon dress, but for some reason struggled. Her hands were shaking. Jason came to her rescue and the dress fell into a sandy pile.

'You look so sexy,' he said, eyeing Angel up and down for a moment, in awe of her black stockings and suspenders. He tried to ascertain the colour of her bra and panties. Except for the fact they were a lighter shade, he didn't really care, he was only interested in what lay beneath. He ripped off his shirt, several buttons flying off in the process, then fumbled for his belt and flies.

Angel stood there giggling.

'Why are you laughing?' asked Jason.

'Sorry,' said Angel, 'I can't help it.'

If truth be known, it was a nervous giggle of anticipation.

By this time Angel was unclipping her bra and teased Jason for a second or two, before releasing her breasts to gravity. She relaxed back onto the sands and started stroking her nipples, encircling each one with the motion of her tongue round her moist lips.

Jason finally managed to yank down his trousers and jockey shorts.

Standing completely starkers against the silhouetted moonlight, Angel could visibly see the growing excitement in him.

Kneeling between Angel's legs, Jason slipped off her panties.

Angel was purring now, like one of the cats in the street, who's just had a belly full of chips.

Jason eased himself on top and made straight for the breasts with his tongue. Flicking tentatively with the same circling motion as Angel's mouth, her nipples erecting like pyramids in the desert. The grains of sand, were sticking to them like glue, from the sweating glands, and the roughness to Angel's skin, brought on a whole new level of excitement in her.

Angel found his mouth again. Her hands reached round to his bum as he slid inside her, pressing herself so urgently against him. Rhythmically like the waves to the shore, they made love. All their inhibitions were lost, lost in the stars.

The night was racing now and the sea retreating. The warm sultry air made the lovers sleepy as they idled into sweet dreams.

Angel was awoken by the tickling seas lapping at her feet, returning from a far off dream. The sun was beginning to rise on the horizon. A new day dawning. Briefly she forgot where she was, but sudden memories came flooding back, as the tide reached her ankles. She looked around anxiously for her love. She peered into the early morning mist, burning off the sea in vapours. The yellow sun doing its magic once again.

'Jason, Jason,' she cried urgently.

Tears began forming in her eyes. Where was he?

Just then, she spied something in the water, bobbing like a seal watching from a safe distance. A silhouette raised from the adoring sea against the sun.

'Angel, Angel, over here,' came the reply.

Angel was soon splashing in the cool waters, still in her stockings and suspenders. The distance between the lovers shortened drastically as they made towards each other. Luckily for Jason, just at a shallow enough depth to stand in, as Angel smothered him once more, wrapping her legs around his waist, otherwise he might have drowned.

'Don't leave me,' ravished Angel between kisses.

'I'm never going to leave you,' Jason replied, 'I love you.'

The lovers melted away, into the blistering heat of another day. This was going to be a long hot summer.

DISTANT DREAMS
Martin C Davis

Once upon a lonely time
Another tale, another rhyme
A beautiful girl that only I can see
She travels far, but only with me
She's in my dreams and in my head
Every night I go to bed
She knows nothing of my existence
Yet our regular meetings know of no distance
Always living on a higher plane
This is my dream and I'm not insane!

This girl so sweet

Her heart is like a golden penny
This girl so sweet, her name is Jenny
With eyes so blue and skin so fair
Long and blonde is her soft silky hair
She lives in her fantasy looking for love
Maybe she just needs a little shove
Though her fiction's addiction her life is so dull
So much work that it's almost full
Working hard to earn her keep
For it is no wonder that she needs her sleep
Working in the city diner
Where the crocks are made of fine bone china
Packed with all those hungry people
As they eat she climbs the steeple
They call her over to clear their plates
They must all think that she wears skates
Then the people stand and leave
An empty room with dirty tables
It's enough to make you want to grieve
And the horses look on as they rest in their stables
Sometimes it's good, sometimes it's bad
I did it too when I was a lad

The diner soon closes
No wine and no roses
Walking home in a blustery gale
Feeling cold, her face is pale
A gecko runs across a littered street
In search of food for a little treat
The street echoes to the sound of rain
The clicking of her shoes as she walks on in vain
The darkness lifted by an ember street lamp
Where in a doorway there sleeps a tramp
Arriving home now safe and sound
She brews a pot and stirs it round
I hear the pouring of the tea
A splash of milk but no sugar for me!
As she starts to unwind thoughts spin through her mind
Reflecting on her day now done
The same tomorrow but where's the fun?
A sudden yawn so far from dawn
I think it may be time for bed
Perchance to dream after the book she read
Travelling far beyond the world of dreams
Where time is endless, or so it seems
Then I see this bright light, an amazing sight
An open door, she'll discover some more

His name is Jack

The best man ever in the pack
This is her man, his name is Jack
He stands tall and proud
His voice so silent yet so loud
So young is he at 23
And very cute, a bit like me!
Jenny I think is a little older
Her birthday scribbled upon my folder
Now back to this man
I'm his number one fan

So sexy is he it makes me sick
His jet black hair is nice and thick
His skin is pure and oh so dark
Just so perfect and unmarked
'Tis a natural hazel colour that compliments those piercing eyes
So dark and deep like lazy autumn skies
He always wears his black T-shirt
If he were mine I'd never flirt
Big veiny arms just brushed with hair
Thick jet black as I stand and stare
His body hair just wreaks of sex
His veins stand out like long thick flex
Pumping blood with all its might
For this is a real man that could win any fight
A tattoo I've seen stamped on his thigh
So green with envy as I give out a sigh
Clean shaven and built with such muscle
Outside a tree sways to a gentle rustle
He wears a ring upon his nipple
It sends out vibes, it creates a ripple
So well toned yet such a gent
I can almost taste his masculine scent
I do not know of Jack and his history
So let him remain a bit of a mystery

Now let me take you by the hand
And show you this place in which we will land
A brand new dimension in which to explore
A change of direction that will not be a bore
Jenny is sleeping but I can't hear her snore
Are you ready to join their dream?
And to witness any change of scene?
Then let us go quietly so far and beyond
Where an angel will wave her magical wand
The place that we land in will know of no evil
A heavenly place and a smile on her face

Close your eyes and clear your mind
And soon you will reach those magical skies
Recall upon when you were young
And how the feeling was oh so strong
Your soul now travelling through the passage of time
Where in this land it is so fine
Left in time like a forgotten book
How I just yearn to take a look
As I turn each and every tattered page
Together forever as I watch them age
This wizard did cast the perfect spell
Hidden deep inside a wishing well
As her dream deepens, reality weakens
Exploring whist snoring
This dream will never be boring

Perchance to dream

They walk along an empty beach
For he has got so much to teach
The golden softness of the sand
They walk together hand in hand
She suddenly stands to listen
As she watches the sea with its glisten
Standing to attention
She turns to see her man of perfection
And as she admires, he sees her desires
You know that all that she knows is a feeling that flows
For these two souls now share the same goals
Speaking words of golden silence
The dream will offer protection and guidance
Those burning rays that shine from the sun
With each new day there's so much fun
Encaptured by some magical power
Their love it blossoms just like a flower
I see their smiles for miles and miles
And watch them spinning, always winning

True happiness you know was found
And their troubles, they're so deep they're underground
They never argue and they never fight
But on sleepless nights her reality bites

It began to grow dark when they walked through the park
The birds were singing and some church bells were ringing
Collecting logs to build a fire
Fully aware of the others' desire
Their lips meet and they began to touch
This power of love is much too much
The crisp down leaves litter the autumn park
But who really cares when love creates that burning spark?

Suddenly faced with a change of scene
It happens quite often in our dreams
Both now on the fun-filled fayre
The wind is captured within their hair
A dozen little angels dance gaily around them
And the children join in from their invisible playpen
Two butterflies put on a show just for their eyes
And tonight he'll have another surprise!

After they fed it was soon time for bed
As they undressed, their clothes thrown in a mess
Bonded together, forever and ever
The smell of his skin drives the passion within
They make love in the night
So sensual, so right
He holds her so tight till when it gets light
So deep in her dream as her fantasy beams
Speaking words of golden silence
The dream will offer protection and guidance

With a crash and a bang it's back to her hell
Suddenly woken by the alarm bell!
Still in a daze into the morning haze
For the dream is now broken since she was woken

For it's time to wake up
And put on some make-up
As a thousand white petals are blown gently away
I know in my heart that his love will stay
I find the strength to let him go
It's a kind of release where I can find peace
Each little petal tells its tale
Then blown form the trees in a mighty gale
The blossom falls in the change of season
Quite simple really, it stands to reason
But when he leaves her heart just grieves
She dies and dies a thousand times
Oh the pain she feels
It's in her face and in her eyes
Now fully awake and at last out of bed
She'll soon be at work
To pick up her thread
Coating her face with a layer of powder
The traffic outside just keeps getting louder
The make-up she wears disguises her pain
And the passion for him that burns like a flame
She sprays on some perfume
It helps lift her gloom
A fragrance quite sweet
And her hair that looks neat
All that she dreams of is all she can't get
The rain is still pouring
She's bound to get wet
Although she's awake
No time for a break
She tidies her skirt
Though you know she's no flirt
She thinks of him and she's hurt
And on the wall she sees some dirt
Not in the flow though she knows she must go

Her day at work

It must have been around half-past eight
When Jenny left and closed the gate
For yet another lonely day
Still as dull and still as grey
This girl I project I'd just love to protect
Waiting endlessly for the bus
Her friend walks by, his name is Gus
He doesn't acknowledge
Like the friendship's abolished
Staring into nothingness all dressed in her gear
She's feeling nostalgic, she's had a tough year
Buried deep beneath so many different thoughts
Wishing that the days could be so short
The bus arrived late but to her it's no fuss
Surrounded by hustle and a few voices rustle
In the midst of the smoke
She's lost in her hope
Her stomach is tangled and twisted like rope

Arriving at work to earn half a crown
Jenny looks on and already she frowns
The time was 10.30
The restaurant still dirty
With tables to move and the bread still to prove
As she starts cleaning she questions life's meaning
She washes the cups, though she must hurry up
If only life was on her side
She could smile and enjoy the ride
The restaurant now open and fully in trading
Her dream has now gone
Or at least slightly fading
The diner soon fills
So many different bills that she will write
If only she could re-live last night
So many faces to be fed
I feel for her as she shakes her head

She clears a table though she feels unable
Her life almost crashes
Watching a plate as it smashes
It fell from her hands and onto the floor
The time had stood still like a slow-motion fall
As the pieces lay scattered across a marbled floor
She imagined her own life and how it all seemed
So broken, battered and torn
She fell to a chair and pulled at her hair
And wondered if he even cares
As she began to cry she asked herself why
For if this is love then at least let it live
For always they'll be so much to give
Alone in a daze
Her eyes are a glaze
She soon feels ready to plough through the day steady
The rush of the lunch time has now passed
Again in the evening will the pace get fast

In the blink of an eye it's turned half-past five
And the world outside soon comes alive
The restaurant gets busy
And again feeling dizzy
Talking to guests is a part of her duty
She offers a smile to enlighten her style
But confuses an order
She treads a fine border
Through the passage of time
Sees the drinking of wine
Soon thy day will endyth
If only her broken heart would mendyth
Thank goodness that her day is finally over
Let us wish upon a four-leaf clover
Standing in a shower of rain

For no one likes to feel the pain
In my heart she's torn apart
But once she's home, she'll be alone
Arriving home I hear my phone
Pouring out her cup of cocoa
It seems to be her magic potion
Her mind still driving
Like a never-ending loco-motion
Yet again it's time for bed
She's feeling tired
She'll rest her head
Jack is waiting and he'll be there
To show this woman how much he cares
Drifting off for yet another night
For this feeling you know she cannot fight
About to turn another page
She wants this dream to be her cage
The page is now turning
Their love is still burning
We may all be sat here and screaming
But turn over this page
Cos Jenny is now dreaming!

The dream was so brief

Dreaming sweetly, so sweetly of him
Living a lie, a lie filled with sin
Together at last is her blast from the past
Gold dust falls from a fantasy sky
And in our dreams we never ask why
Dancing to music and its heavenly beat
A perfect love in a perfect world
Such a beautiful place to find your retreat
She must be absurd as I dream and observe
The dream was so brief
Unlike the falling of a dying autumn leaf
I watch it fall as she yells out for more

I see snow and ice
And a child rolls a dice
As glistening snowflakes are scattered around
The silence is golden
Hush, not a sound
Silence is a distant beat
A beating heart and two tiny feet
Silence left behind a closing door
Her eyes shut tight as she yearns for some more

I watch them go skating
Her angel's awaiting
Still fast asleep, for this dream she will keep
She wriggles and giggles as they visit some dairy
A lady called Mary and two tiny fairies offer good luck
She'll never want to close this book
Dancing through time so sweet and divine
'Twas all in her mind for the dream was too kind
Time had stood still when it was just turning two
The clock gave its chime in its usual rhyme
And wide awake for goodness sake
The clock in the background with its tick and its tock
Alone she stands and in the dock
Feeling cold, the night unfolds
Her loneliness is hurting me
If only I could set her free

Now close your eyes and count again
These words I write I need my pen
Leaping through so many skies
Together again but by no surprise
Back in her dream where he crowns her his queen
Her knighthood was honoured by pure love and devotion
Such feelings run high
Just like the emotion
Now coated in glitter
This dream has no litter

Committing their crimes as they dance through the times
Around goes the wine and everything's fine
But waking from her heavenly spell
This feeling of loneliness she knows so well
She struggles and fights to hold onto this night
But as she awakes her dream all but brakes
She remembered the plate as it crashed to the floor
Her own life so broken, battered and torn
Sitting to eat some humble pie
She looks upon the moonlit sky
As the sequins fall her bubble has burst
Where is this man to quench her thirst?
Starting to weep sends her to sleep
Turning the page of this story still strong
This is my song though it's nearly sung
She sleeps in my heart so silent and still
For she knows of no part that she wishes to kill
As I see many pictures of their lives and their fixtures
Learning to love in all of life's mixtures
The joy so intense
No need for pretence

Another night to lay to rest
She feels the pain within her chest
Another day of toil and trouble
I need a drink - make mine a double!
A day ahead of work and chores
Why does life feel such a bore?
Wanting to escape from her perils of duty
She lives in her dream cos she knows of its beauty
Starring as she holds her drink
A tap sits tightly on the kitchen sink
Drops of water fall slowly with a gentle splash
Unlike the plate with its almighty crash
She grasps so tightly to her scented rose
Where in the midst of time the scene was froze
The petals fall beneath her toes
For this is her life and all that she knows

A photo of Jack is held in her mind
It lifts her day when life's unkind
The distant ringing of the phone
Seems like the lights are on but no one's home

'Twas simply a dream

Flirting with thoughts within her mind
Her watch, as she glanced, just needs a wind
This lonely day so filled with grey
A falling bouquet that lands in the hay
Unaware of what lies ahead
As she shakes the quilt upon her bed
A phoenix rises from the ashes
Late for work, she runs and she dashes

Arriving at work to earn her crust
She calls upon the dream now gone and turned to rust
Floating on some lonesome cloud
Boy, when she screams, she screams out loud
The thoughts still spinning around her head
And just so wanting to be tucked up in bed
A chill ran down her tingling spine
And in her dream they both drank wine
From coast to coast she feels his ghost
Cos the dream you know she cannot touch
But how she loves him so very much

The restaurant was open and the people flocked in
A mistake on a page that I threw in the bin
The typewriter clatters to an amazing beat
The story near the endyth, it's really quite sweet
Now back in the diner is where we will find her
A party of twelve who were sat in the window
Having a laugh over a colleague's new lingo
So many different voices
And then life with its choices

Talking on the telephone
Still feeling all alone
Speaking to a man I think called Jim
Didn't seem to matter when the door flew open and some guy walked in
A silence so sudden that it's almost a sin
For when she turned
She knew it was him
A storm erupted within her belly
She soon felt sick and turned to jelly
He looked the same as in her dream
So pure, so sweet and oh, so clean
Her heart must have skipped a thousand beats
This girl so in love who avoids all the cheats
They stood face to face
Her heart beating to a faster pace
Words were not spoken
Footsteps were not taken
But I know her nerves were fairly shaken!
So much chemistry had taken over
As he handed her that four-leaf clover
She was just so overcome by so much joy
As she continued to stare at this dream lover boy
Will this end in a grand love affair?
As the crowd in the restaurant continue their stares
Standing there she began to shake . . .
. . . The end for now as I awake
Drinking coffee with a little cream
Didn't I tell you it was simply *my dream?*

OUT FOR A DUCK
Maddie Bourke

'How's *zat,*' was the cry that Peter Bowler heard as he watched a fielder jump in the air with excitement after catching the first ball he'd struck with his cricket bat. *Damn I made a right bloody hash of that,* Peter thought to himself. So much for me trying to be a flash b*****d. That won't impress anyone especially her. Who he meant by her was a girl he'd been watching earlier when he'd been fielding. One of the opposing players had hit a six causing the ball to land in her lap knocking the book she was reading out of her hands. Peter ran over to retrieve the ball, he threw the ball back to one of the other fielders then he picked up the girl's book and handed it to her.

'Are you alright?' Peter enquired.

'Oh yes thanks. It just startled me that's all, no harm done.'

'Sorry about that,' said Peter.

'Don't be silly it wasn't your fault.'

'Hey Peter are you playing cricket or chatting up the ladies?'

'Sorry just coming.' But in the brief meeting Peter couldn't help noticing just how stunningly beautiful the girl was. She had the most gorgeous hazel brown eyes he had ever clapped his eyes on and her long brown hair that she wore in a ponytail was just as stunning. *I wouldn't mind taking her out one evening. I'd really impress the lads with her on my arm,* thought Peter.

The rest of the opposing side's innings Peter made a complete mess of fielding, dropping a couple of easy catches.

'Butter fingers pull your socks up,' one of his team-mates shouted.

Peter couldn't concentrate on the game at all as he found his eyes constantly watching the girl with the hazel eyes. He couldn't help noticing her perfectly shaped breasts as just enough of her cleavage was revealed from the white cotton summer dress she was wearing, that was held up by two thin straps of white silk over her shoulders. He couldn't get a view of her legs as the dress was ankle length but a small delicate sandalled foot protruded from the bottom of the dress showing a perfectly shaped sun-tanned ankle with a small gold chain around it. The more Peter looked over at her the more beautiful she appeared to him.

Peter tucked his bat under his left arm and started walking towards the pavilion. Out for a duck, just my luck. I bet she thinks I'm a proper twit. Peter carried on walking towards the pavilion not taking his eyes off the girl and almost walking into one of the white posts that held up the front of the pavilion. Peter went inside and took off his gloves and leg pads still determined to try his luck with the girl, but when he came out of the pavilion the seat that the girl had been occupying was empty and there was no sign of her.

'Pint of lager please Godfrey,' requested Peter to the barman in the clubhouse.

'You played like a second rate amateur boy,' said a voice in a strong Welsh accent, 'I bet you don't play that bad when you play for the county. In fact we all know you don't. You've let the whole village down Peter boy so you have.'

'Sorry Shadwell everyone has their off days, what can I say, come on have a pint on me.'

'I've never been known to refuse a pint but that doesn't excuse you from playing like a second rate schoolboy, and don't think I didn't notice you watching that girl instead of concentrating on what you should have been doing, for example playing cricket for this village.'

'Yes guilty,' replied Peter holding his hand up in the air.

'I ruddy well knew it,' Shadwell butted in.

'Alright but who was she?' pleaded Peter.

'I've never clapped eyes on her before but Mrs Evans said that she was one of the Vicar's daughters. Katrina I think she said her name was. Just come up from London to see her parents. Apparently she's been studying at some big university down there.'

'Thanks Shadwell you're a brick,' smile Peter then he swallowed his pint down in one and left the clubhouse.

Peter walked across the village green to where he had parked his red MG sports car, rolled back the open roof and sped off towards the village church. As he turned down the lane that led to his destination he saw her walking down the lane making him brake to a sudden halt. Her beauty took his breath away. Peter just sat there watching her as the sun shone down through the leaves of the trees. They seemed to make an archway as they grew on each side of the lane making the sun's rays glisten on her hazelnut brown hair and revealing a beautiful perfect shaped body through the thin white cotton summer dress. *What chance have I got of asking a Goddess like that to go out with me? She'll laugh in my face as soon as I ask,* Peter thought to himself. Then he reversed the car back up the lane, did a three-point turn deciding that he'd just have to carry on dreaming.

Katrina's father was sat on one of the benches in the churchyard writing one of his sermons when Katrina approached and sat down next to her father.

'Oh hello Katrina, had a nice day?'

'Yes thanks Daddy I've been down to the village watching the cricket match on the village green.'

'You do like your cricket don't you Katrina, was it a good match?'

'Not bad,' Katrina told her father, 'but the star player for the village didn't play very well, at least I was told he was their star player before the match started.'

'What did he look like?' asked her father.

'Oh, tall with blue eyes, extremely good looking.'

'Sounds like you were more interested in him than the cricket,' smiled her father.

'Oh Daddy!' Katrina blushed, 'I only noticed him because he picked up my book for me when a cricket ball knocked it out of my hand.'

Katrina's father turned towards her and put her hand in his, 'His name is Peter Bowler and he's a professional county player. Would you like to meet him Katrina dear?'

Katrina went bright red. 'You mean you don't mind introducing me Daddy?'

'Oh I don't see why not. He seems a nice young man and he's the same age as you, I'll see what I can do.'

'Thanks Daddy but I only want to meet him to talk about cricket and to ask him why he played so badly today.'

'Of course you do,' her father smiled. 'I don't know him personally but I'm a great friend of his father, in fact I'm going to ring him to ask if he'd like to play a round of golf with me after tomorrow morning's service.'

Then her father went into the vicarage to make his phone call, leaving Katrina sat on the bench with her thoughts.

So his name's Peter, that's a nice name, thought Katrina. He looks magnificent in his whites. Those gorgeous blue eyes and that cheeky grin he gave me when he gave me my book back. He's just dreamy with that lovely ash blond hair he must have all the girls for miles around chasing him. I bet he never gave me a second thought after he walked away. After all what could he see in me, a plain old vicar's daughter.

Peter slumped onto the couch in his father's study. 'I played like a right chump today Dad. There was this gorgeous girl watching the match and I couldn't take my eyes off her. I later found out that she was your friend the vicar's daughter.' But before he could finish telling his father the whole tale the phone rang.

'Tell me after I answer the phone son.' Then his father picked up the receiver, 'Hello, Chris Bowler speaking, oh hello James are you well?' The vicar then asked Chris if he'd like to have a game of golf with him after tomorrow's service. 'Why I'd love to James just as long as you don't sulk again, you'll never get the better of me you know.'

'I know that Chris, but it's a great help playing a professional like you.'

'Just as long as you understand.'

'By the way Chris my daughter was watching your Peter play cricket this morning and I think she's a little smitten with him, is there any chance that she might meet him some time?'

'Oh I think there's every chance. In fact aren't you having a sixties dance at the parish hall this evening. I think my wife was telling me.'

'Oh yes, your wife said that you both might attend but I didn't want to push you, if you know what I mean Chris.'

'I can assure you James, me and the wife will be there with Peter by our side,' laughed Peter's father, 'Goodbye James.'

Peter's father put the phone back down on its base. 'That was the vicar I was talking to.'

'I gathered that but what was all that nonsense about us all going to an old sixties dance, you and Mum might be, but you can leave me out. All I need after a day like this is an old sixties dance. Sorry Dad forget it.'

Peter's father chuckled. 'Not even if a girl called Katrina wants to meet you there. Go and get yourself smartened up Peter, we'll be leaving about eight.'

SEASONS IN LOVE
Kathleen Townsley

He watched her as she arrived onto his private beach, every day for three weeks he had been going to remove her from his property, but something held him back, maybe it was the wind blowing through his hair, or the sun as it highlighted the deep mahogany curls against the nape of her neck, whatever it was it stopped him from calling out. I think he was also a little scared that he might frighten her, for sitting on the beach she looked so vulnerable, a little lost, yet determination was there in her walk as she left each day at 2pm, she arrived at twelve noon and sat on the large rock staring out to sea. He was certain she was unaware of what she was eating on her sandwiches for her eyes just kept on staring out to sea, as if she was searching the waves for a long lost glimpse of a passing ship, hoping against hope that it would stop and take her away from this place, but as 2pm approached she would shrug her shoulders, collect the wrappings from her lunch and walk straight off the beach without a backward glance.

At first when he saw her, he was annoyed, this was his beach, his place of solitude, but as time went by he became obsessed with the girl, he did not say those words lightly, for indeed he had become obsessed, for how else could he explain the re-arranging of his appointments over the past two weeks just so he could be at home for 11.45am, to sit here at the window and await her arrival, *yes,* he said to himself, *a definite obsession.* Today he had made up his mind to speak to the girl, and was awaiting her arrival with growing dread, for he knew this move could send her away for good, he had given it great thought and had decided to accidentally meet her as she stepped down onto the beach, this was easily done for he had brought his dog Autumn with him. She was so named due to the browns and golds in her coat as she ran through the sunshine, a mongrel he had found left on the beach, but to him she was a pure pedigree, and although he told her she was the second in command, just one look from those brown eyes and his heart lurched and she got whatever she wished, be it a bone or a nice warm seat on the settee. He was watching her bound along the beach chasing her ball, smiling as the sun played with her fur causing a kaleidoscope of autumn colours to explode with each leap and bound when a gentle voice said, 'She is so lovely, is she yours?'

Turning he looked into the widest pair of brown eyes, again his heart lurched, 'Yes,' he stuttered, 'she is mine.'

'What is her name?'

'Autumn,' he managed to say, then realising he was staring at her like a complete idiot, turned to watch Autumn running along the beach.

'A season like me,' she said, 'my name is Summer.'

Turning to look at her again he knew why, for the sun was again playing with the curls that hung gently about her face.

As he turned back towards the beach he saw Autumn lying by the rock, he called her name but she did not move, the next thing he knew he was knelt at her side, how he got there he did not know. 'What is the matter girl,' he said looking into her sad brown eyes.

'Please move to one side and let me see, maybe I can help, I am a vet.' As if in a dream he moved to kneel beside Autumn's head, and watched as the young woman gently examined Autumn, 'I see the problem Autumn,' she said, and very gently lifted her back leg up, that is when he saw the blood.

'Oh God,' he said, the young woman kept her eyes on Autumn, finally she looked at the man kneeling beside his dog, such deep worry lines on his face, 'She will be fine, a very clever girl is Autumn, she had stood on some broken glass and this is embedded in her paw, if she had continued walking, we would have been in serious trouble, if you will kindly carry her to my car I will gladly take you both back to the surgery and attend to her leg.' Lifting Autumn into his arms, he did as she asked, and paced the waiting room when she had taken Autumn into the inner sanctum. It seemed an age before the door opened and in walked the young woman carrying Autumn in her arms, 'She is fine, a little groggy for I have had to give her a light sedative to enable me to clean the wound. She has had six stitched in the wound, and must be watched for the next three days.' Seeing the worry lines appear on the man's face she quickly said, 'Only to make sure she does not remove the dressing, I hope to see her in seven days, when hopefully the stitches can be removed. That is, unless you wish to take her to your own veterinary surgery.'

'No,' said the man, 'you have been wonderful, I cannot thank you enough, you have saved her life and I will be forever in your debt.'

Smiling she said, 'I do not think it was as serious as that and as for being in my debt, I think my bill will soon change that.' Then smiling she said, 'If you take Autumn to my car I will take you both home, where is that?'

'The beach house,' said the man.

He carried Autumn into the house and offered Summer a cup of tea and maybe some lunch for he knew she had missed lunchtime, through saving Autumn's life, he realised he had said the last bit out loud.

'Hardly,' she said with a smile, 'but I will accept a tea from you and maybe a seat at your table so I can eat my sandwiches,' that was the least he could do for her, he felt totally in her debt, for he knew where Autumn was concerned he would not have been able to help her, for seeing her lying there on the beach took any sense he had in his brain and blew it right away, and all he could do was ask her stupid questions like what's the matter girl. Over lunch they chatted away and he told Summer that he would see to the broken bottle and make sure it never happened again. This was put into operation as soon as Summer left, within two days a fence had been built around the beach area belonging to beach house and a strong lock was placed on the gate leading to the walkway to the house, all was secure. It was on the third day as he was watching Autumn sniff around her bandage when the doorbell rang. As he walked to the front door he called behind him to Autumn, to 'leave that bandage alone or I will be angry with you and there will be no treats.'

'I do not believe that,' said the gentle voice. Turning, he saw that Summer was standing on his doorstep. 'I was just passing and wondered how the invalid was, but I can see she is much better,' this being said as Summer fell to her knees to hug Autumn, who in return was giving her big kisses.

'I think you have a fan there,' he said.

'Only one,' she said. 'Do you know if the fence around the beach is going to stay or is it only till the beach has been cleaned due to Autumn's accident?'

'It is staying,' said the man.

'I thought so, I have only just learned that this is a private beach, I thought it was for public use, and have enjoyed coming down here every day to have my lunch. It was nice to get away from work, and to watch the changing seasons,' turning the man handed her a box from off the table. It was small and had a pink ribbon tied around, opening the box she found a key.

Looking up at the man in bewilderment he said, 'That is a key to Autumn's beach. You are welcome here anytime.'

Summer looked at the man and said, 'This is yours,' the man nodded, 'oh I am so sorry for trespassing before,' said Summer, 'and thank you Autumn for allowing me to share your glorious beach, I will gladly accept this key,' and kneeling down she received a further face full of kisses. Standing and holding out her hand to the man she said, 'Summer Livingston.'

'Patrick Winters,' said the man, all through lunch they chatted away, then before she left, agreed on a time for Patrick to return to the surgery with Autumn.

As he was leaving the surgery following Autumn's removal of her stitches Summer said, 'Thank you for letting me spend time on the beach, in return I wondered if you would like to have supper with me one evening, well you and Autumn.'

'We would love to,' he answered, following the usual hugs and kisses for Autumn he said, 'she is one lucky girl in more ways than one,' then thanking Summer he left the surgery, only to find when he arrived at the car he had forgotten to pay the bill. Returning to the surgery he saw the door was open into the inner sanctum, as he was going to call out he heard Summer say, 'How do you know him then?'

'He is one of the surgeons who saw to my Molly following her accident, one of the top surgeons at the veterinary hospital in the city, well respected and may I say well admired by all the nurses, but as far as I am aware he remains single.'

Patrick turned and quietly left the surgery, he would pay the bill later.

A few days later when he returned from a busy day at the hospital he found a note waiting behind the front door. After feeding Autumn, who was always hungry after all the fussing she got at the hospital he looked at the letter. This he thought is the sorry I cannot arrange for the dinner yet, due to the extra work load at present. This he found happened a lot. Some women were afraid to look behind the surgeon's face. He had prayed Summer had been different, or they wanted to impress their friends with their latest catch. This is why he had given up on women and put all his efforts into his skills as a surgeon.

Sitting at the table later that evening watching the sun going down over the horizon, he opened the note. He read aloud, 'I hope you don't mind a short notice, but tomorrow would suit me fine if you are free that is.' She had given her address and phone number and asked him to give a big kiss to Autumn. 'As I said before, you are a lucky girl,' he told Autumn, planting the requested kiss on the top of her head, then picking up the phone he rang Summer's number. It was well after 9pm when he came off the phone and it was only due to Autumn asking to go out for her evening walk that had caused the disconnection, for he was certain he could have talked to Summer all night, and judging by her response she felt the same way. 'Maybe,' he said to Autumn, 'the seasons we both love dearly, will become seasons in love.'

Whilst down in her cottage Summer thought, *I have always wanted a spring wedding, and spring would make it complete.*

INFORMATION

We hope you have enjoyed reading this book - and that you will continue to enjoy it in the coming years.

If you are interested in becoming a New Fiction author then drop us a line, or give us a call, and we'll send you a free information pack.

Alternatively if you would like to order further copies of this book or any of our other titles, then please give us a call or log onto our website at www.forwardpress.co.uk

New Fiction Information
Remus House
Coltsfoot Drive
Peterborough
PE2 9JX
(01733) 898101